T0267858

I Was Told There Would Be ROMANCE

I WAS TOLD THERE WOULD BE ROMANCE

MARIE ARNOLD

LITTLE, BROWN AND COMPANY
New York Boston

Copyright © 2024 by Marie Arnold

Flower ornament art copyright © Vitalino11/Shutterstock.com; envelope art copyright © meookami/Shutterstock.com

Cover art copyright © 2024 by Mimi Moffie. Cover design by Patrick Hulse. Cover copyright © 2024 by Hachette Book Group, Inc. Interior design by Michelle Gengaro-Kokmen.

Little, Brown and Company
Hachette Book Group
1290 Avenue of the Americas, New York, NY 10104
Visit us at LBYR.com

First Edition: October 2024

Little, Brown and Company is a division of Hachette Book Group, Inc. The Little, Brown name and logo are registered trademarks of Hachette Book Group, Inc.

The publisher is not responsible for websites (or their content) that are not owned by the publisher.

Little, Brown and Company books may be purchased in bulk for business, educational, or promotional use. For information, please contact your local bookseller or the Hachette Book Group Special Markets Department at special.markets@hbgusa.com.

Library of Congress Cataloging-in-Publication Data
Names: Arnold, Marie, author.
Title: I was told there would be romance / Marie Arnold.
Description: First edition. | New York : Little, Brown and Company, 2024. | Audience: Ages 12 & up. | Summary: Fifteen-year-old Haitian American Fancy navigates high school, friendship, and crushes.
Identifiers: LCCN 2023051676 | ISBN 9780316568005 (hardcover) | ISBN 9780316568029 (ebook)
Subjects: CYAC: Interpersonal relations—Fiction. | Friendship—Fiction. | High schools—Fiction. | Schools—Fiction. | Haitian Americans—Fiction. | LCGFT: Novels.
Classification: LCC PZ7.1.A7632 Iaw 2024 | DDC [Fic]—dc23
LC record available at https://lccn.loc.gov/2023051676

ISBNs: 978-0-316-56800-5 (hardcover), 978-0-316-56802-9 (ebook)

Printed in Indiana, USA

LSC-C

Printing 1, 2024

This book is dedicated to Mike & Lo,
the first characters to teach me about true love.
And to romance lovers everywhere, of all ages.

CHAPTER 1

"I'm not a stalker," I assure my school counselor. She looks at me from across her desk and nods in a way that leads me to think she may not completely believe me. She starts talking, but I tune her out; something has changed in her office. The poster behind Mrs. Washington, of kids playing on a sunny beach, has been moved about six inches to the left.

"You moved that poster."

"I think it's better where it is now," she replies.

I nod and try to forget about it. I can't. I find my eyes darting between where the poster is and where it used to be. Now that it's been moved, the room feels wrong.

Mrs. Washington studies me, sighs, and says, "Would you like me to move it back to where it was?"

I shrug. "Only if you want to."

She gets up and moves the poster back to its original place. Everything is okay again.

"Now, where was I?" I ask.

"Stalking," Mrs. Washington replies.

"Oh, yeah, I'm not a stalker," I say with renewed conviction.

Mrs. Washington clasps her hands together and eyes me with mounting suspicion. I wonder what it's like being her. I'm sure she has a charmed life; I think all pretty people do. Mrs. Washington has delicate features, a straight perm, and dark skin. She's basically a Black Barbie doll.

Me, on the other hand, I'm Barbie's curvy, big-breasted, natural-haired distant cousin. You know, the kind of doll that's giant compared to the small, dainty ones on the shelf? The one whose hair never stays on her head because the manufacturer didn't take the time to fit it properly? That's me—off-brand Barbie.

"You do realize that most of our conversations start out with you telling me all the things that you aren't?" she says.

"All of them? I doubt that."

She opens her cabinet and takes out a green folder with my name clearly printed on the front: Falencia Marie Augustine. She takes a look inside the folder and then looks back at me.

"Fancy, the last time you were in my office, it was because you failed to hand in several homework assignments for Mr. Doyle. You started out by saying, 'I'm not a slacker.' The time before that, you were in here because you were caught in the boys' locker room. You started that meeting by saying, 'I'm not a pervert.'"

"I admit, I'm a little behind on schoolwork. I'm working on it," I say. "And as for the locker room thing, it was an innocent mistake. I was reading this romance book called *The Many Loves of Lucy Luckless* and got so into it, I walked into the wrong locker room."

"And once you found yourself in the boys' locker room, did you quickly scurry out or linger?" she asks me.

I bite my lower lip. "Define *linger*...."

She groans with disapproval. "And what about today? Why did I catch you following Rahim at lunch?"

I raise my eyebrow suggestively. "Mrs. Washington, we *both* know why I followed Rahim...."

Rahim Robinson is a yummy, chocolate-covered knight, filled with a gooey center. Normally I don't like describing a Black person's complexion using food, but in this case, it's apt. Rahim was blessed with searing, dark-brown bedroom eyes, a sculpted jawline, and full, kissable lips. He's on the basketball team, where his tall, athletic build is displayed for all to adore. He swaggers down the school halls like he has the answers to questions the universe hasn't even thought to ask.

"Fancy, you have to stop following Rahim!" Mrs. Washington insists.

"Don't worry, I always keep a safe 'tailing distance' the whole time. He never knows I'm there," I reply proudly.

"That's not the reassurance I was looking for."

"And for the record, other girls follow him around, too," I reply.

"None of them follows him inside the locker room!"

"Well, obviously, they lack dedication," I mumble.

She smiles but quickly catches herself and goes back to "adult mode." She clears her throat and straightens her posture.

"I won't deny that Rahim is a handsome young man. But following him is unacceptable. Have you ever considered just *talking* to him?"

"How do you talk to a god?"

"I know that drama and hormones are the fuel on which high school runs, but Fancy, we're only a few weeks into the school year. Pace yourself," she pleads.

"I'll try."

"You need to start focusing on your work—in every class, not just in English, where you excel. And you need to stop going along with every whim that hits you."

"Like what?" I ask, insulted.

"Well, like the time Imani caught you trying on her bra in the girls' locker room."

"I didn't try it on. I just placed it in front of me to see what it would look like."

She creases her forehead and leans in closer. "You see how that's weird, right?"

"Of course you don't get it," I mutter. "You're part of the bra parade."

She tilts her head, curious. "The what?"

I explain to her that the bra parade is an unofficial event that takes place in the center aisle of the girls' locker room. The girls strut up and down showing off their Insta-worthy bras.

"You can join the parade and strut if you so choose," Mrs. Washington replies.

"Nope! Everyone else's bras are sophisticated, stylish, and distinctly feminine—the kinds of garments delicately crafted by a master seamstress in a quaint boutique in Paris. My bras require a team of structural engineers. They need fewer people to build bridges."

"Fancy, you're making too big a deal about this bra thing."

I scoff. "Spoken like a 34D."

Her jaw drops. "How did you know my—"

I shrug. "It's a gift. And a curse."

She squirms slightly in her chair and then pulls the lapels of her blazer closer together.

"I'm sure you can find places that custom-make pretty bras in your size," she continues.

"Mrs. Washington, there's freedom in being able to get your exact size in any and every store. A freedom I have long been denied," I reply wistfully.

She groans and rolls her eyes hard.

I jump up, eager to be heard. "Pretty. Perky. Perfect. Boobs. That's always been my dream. And we both know what happens to a dream deferred...."

She frowns deeply. "You're not dragging Langston Hughes into this."

"Okay, fine. But for the record, trying on Imani's bra once is not a good enough reason for her to despise me."

"Fancy, you know the way Imani feels about you has nothing to do with the bra situation."

"Yeah, I know. It's the spider...," I lament.

"Yes, the spider."

When I was in third grade, I saw a spider that freaked me out, and I tossed a ball at it. The ball bounced and hit Imani. Her loose tooth fell out; it didn't help that it was picture day....

"It could have happened to anyone."

Mrs. Washington gives me the side-eye. I get it.

"Here's the deal," she says, dragging me out of my thoughts. "You've been coming to my office for one infraction or another way too often. I think it's time I call your parents."

A wave of panic hits me. I feel cold beads of sweat forming on my forehead and upper lip. I try to reassure myself that I didn't hear what I just heard.

"I'm sorry, Mrs. Washington, can you repeat that?"

"You heard me. I remember you telling me that your parents are kind of strict, but I think—"

"*Kind of strict?* North Korean dictators are kind of strict. My parents are *Haitian*! Did you know there's a list of all the places Haitian kids are allowed to go? Lekòl. Legliz. Lakay. That means: School. Church. Home. You would not believe the acts of subterfuge I have to commit just to hang after school."

"Well, you have to— Wait, what subterfuge?" she asks.

Damn.

"Your point is, I've gone too far and I need to pull back. I'm on it. You won't see me in your office again," I promise her.

"I'm not sure you *can* stay out of my office," she replies.

"I totally can! Just promise you won't call my parents. If you call them, it's only a matter of time before they start thinking I've become 'too American' and send me back to Haiti."

"I've heard how rough life can be over there," she replies sadly.

"That's just it: I've gone to Haiti before and it was dope! I ate fresh seafood by the beach, went hiking up resplendent mountains, and drank coconut water right from the coconut."

"If you love it that much, why would you be upset at the thought of getting sent back by your parents?"

"Because 'vacation Haiti' and 'sent-back Haiti' are two very different things," I tell her. She looks at me totally confused. "Simply put, when I go to Haiti on vacation, I note all the good things it has to offer. However, when you get sent back for acting out and disgracing your family... let's just say you start to notice the things Haiti doesn't have—like child labor laws and child protective services."

"I'm pretty sure you're being dramatic. In fact, I'm positive you are," she replies.

"I knew this guy, Jean-Louis. His parents sent him back because he was cutting school and stealing. He thought he was going back to 'vacation Haiti.' But he soon learned about the other version of Haiti. It's a sad tale. I call it 'The Ballad of Jean-Louis.' It's a song I'll never sing. I promise you, Mrs. Washington."

She throws her hands up in defeat. "Okay, I won't call your parents—this time. But if you get sent back to my office—"

"I won't."

"Good. Also, Mr. Doyle tells me you have a report due this week. I expect you to hand that in."

"Yup, I've already started."

She arches her eyebrow. How does she know I'm lying?

"Okay, I started it *in my head*. But it's there, Mrs. Washington. It's in the ether."

"Well, you better get it down on an actual document. Or else."

"I'm on it!"

"Good. Now go on, get out of my office. I have work to do."

"Okay, I'm going," I reply as I gather my things. "Following Rahim around is its own reward, but I have to admit, it's turned parts of my brain into mush. Like today, I almost forgot it's Weeping Wednesday."

Every year, a batch of bright red envelopes with engraved

gold calligraphy circulates around the school. The first year this happened, it was on a Wednesday, hence the name Weeping Wednesday. It's an invitation to the social event of the year—Imani Parker's birthday party. Imani is to our school what Anna Wintour is to the fashion industry. Her birthday party is as exclusive as the Met Gala.

The invite comes to a chosen few, and the ones who don't make it are, in a word, devastated. It's like the scene from *Scarface* where Tony Montana brutally kills everyone—Weeping Wednesday is that, except social lives get slaughtered. Every year, dozens of girls break down in tears because Imani assured them a place, only to find that they've been left out in the cold. Imani and I have gone to the same school since kindergarten. I have never received an envelope, but it would be nice. Actually, it would be more than nice. I heard she has a foyer, perfect for making a grand entrance! I may or may not have pranced around my room countless times, working on my entrance.

Mrs. Washington looks out with dead eyes. "Weeping Wednesday is today? No! It can't be!" she says, shaking her head in pure terror.

"Yeah, it is. This year, Imani has travel plans on her actual birthday, so they're moving up her party date. Invitations are out today. It's all anyone's been able to talk about around here. I'm surprised you missed that," I reply.

"I was swamped with work. This is a nightmare! My office overflowing with emotional girls who won't stop crying.

9

Students demanding to change schools to get away from the stigma of not getting an invite," Mrs. Washington says, clearly traumatized. She runs to the door and swallows hard, as if to gather her courage, before peeking outside. I take a quick look, too. And sure enough, there's a line of devastated students that goes around the corner. They're all waiting to talk to her. Mrs. Washington quickly closes the door and leans against it for support. "I'm not ready."

"Where's your stash?" I ask.

"My what?"

"Your 'break glass in case of emergency' candy. C'mon, everyone on the staff has some."

She looks at me and is about to confess, but at the last moment she shrugs and says, "I don't handle emergency situations by eating my feelings; I handle them with calm thoughts and deep, cleansing breaths."

A girl cries out from the other side of the door, "My life is over!" Loud sobbing quickly follows.

Mrs. Washington says, "It's on the shelf, behind the book titled *School Code of Ethics*."

I look, and sure enough, there's a wrinkled brown paper bag hidden in the corner. I take a peek inside and then hand it over to her. "I'm not upset that you lied to me. I am, however, disappointed that your guilty emergency treat is candy corn," I scold.

She rolls her eyes as she takes the bag from me. She goes

on to pop a handful of candy into her mouth and moans with pleasure as she inhales her sugary escape. Soon she's pouring the contents of the bag straight into her mouth.

I pat her shoulder gently. "Mrs. Washington, we're only a few weeks into the school year—pace yourself."

CHAPTER 2

I walk out of Mrs. Washington's office and down the school hallway. I hear bits and pieces of conversations from the students as I go past. The ones who got the invite squeal with excitement, and the ones who didn't desperately try to recall what they did or said that got them taken off the list.

Suddenly, the chaos and sobbing that comes with Weeping Wednesday stops. All the students turn their heads in the same direction, their expressions ranging from awe to envy. The temperature in the hallway drops by about ten degrees. The sudden chill in the air penetrates to my bones. There's only two ways to explain it: either we are in a Harry Potter book and the Dementors are making an entrance, or Imani and her two sidekicks have arrived.

Imani Parker is a flawless beauty, so much so that her Insta selfies don't require a filter. Her jet-black micro braids fall to her waist and sway side to side. Her dark skin glows, and every color she wears is her color. Everything about her—face, figure, and frame—is impeccable. When you combine that with her family's money, she was almost predestined to be a mean girl.

The two tagalongs on either side of her are Echo and Cheer. Those aren't their real names, but believe me, they're apt. The one on the right of Imani is Echo. All she does is repeat whatever Imani says. She's never had an original thought in her admittedly pretty head. She's also not the brightest girl in the world. But with her mid-length silky faux locs, slim figure, and high cheekbones, she doesn't need to be.

Cheer's there for no other reason than to keep Imani's ego as inflated as possible. She adores Imani almost as much as Imani adores herself. Cheer's hair is styled in big, loose curls and cascades past her shoulders. It's the best lace-front weave I've ever seen. She has an almost supernatural ability to sniff out secrets. And when she does, she takes them straight to Imani and Echo. They fashion that secret into a sharp spear and find some unsuspecting student to harpoon.

The students with invites nod gratefully at the Triad of evil as they sashay by. I'm hoping that maybe, just this once, Imani sees me and hands me an invite. Yeah, I know the chances are small, but still, a girl can dream.

Imani sees me standing off to the side and makes a beeline for me. Wait, could this be it? Am I getting an invite?

"Fancy, you look...disappointed. You weren't expecting to get an invite, were you?"

"Yeah, you weren't expecting that, were you?" Echo adds. I resist the urge to roll my eyes. I shrug and try to play it off.

"Not really," I mumble.

Imani laughs. "Oh, good. The truth is, I can't have you at my party because, well...you're you."

"What does that mean?" I ask before I can stop myself.

The Triad of evil exchanges a laugh. "She means she won't ever invite you because you don't exist," Cheer adds.

"Um, thanks?" I reply sarcastically.

"You're welcome," Cheer says.

"I don't want to be the kind of girl who doesn't help other girls, so I'll give you some advice," Imani says with a smile. "If you ever want to get invited to my parties, you might start with changing your clothes. And then your hair. It won't get you an invite, but it'll be a start."

"You're such a good person to give her advice. A lot of other girls would just let her go on dressing like that," Cheer says.

Imani shrugs. "I believe in giving back."

"Don't worry about me, Imani," I say. "I have plans that night."

She scoffs. "What plans?"

"I'm gonna hang out with my best friend, Tilly. She doesn't

care what I wear or what I look like. You know, a true friend," I add against my better judgment.

Echo chimes in. "Are you saying the three of us aren't really friends? For your information, last year, when Imani had a bad acne breakout and couldn't come to school, both of us stayed home in seniority."

"You mean solidarity?" I ask.

"Yeah, that's what I said. Loser," Echo replies.

"Don't brag about your friendship with that Tilly girl," Imani says. "I'm sure the only reason she's friends with you is because she has no other options. If she did, she'd never even look your way. Just like the rest of us." She then stalks off, looking very pleased with herself.

I used to let Imani's words crush me completely; now any rude remark from her is merely a momentary slight. Yes, an invite would be nice, but I have Tilly Fischer.

And together, we have everything.

"Fancy!" Tilly calls out from in front of our lockers. I make my way over to her. "Was Imani bothering you again?"

I shrug. "Everyone needs a hobby."

Last year, by some miracle, we got lockers right next to each other. But this school year, we had an entire hallway separating us. I had to track down the kid who got my old locker next to Till's. His name is Anderson. He said he would gladly help two best friends stay together—for a small monthly fee. Tilly thinks it's a waste of money and that us being a hallway away isn't a big deal. She's wrong. Besides, we ought to have the same lockers we did freshman year. Continuity is a beautiful thing.

"Forget about Imani. One day she'll be food for worms."

"Aw, you say the sweetest things," I joke.

Tilly is short for Matilda, which she thinks is an awful name for a Black girl. When she says that, I remind her that her dad is white. She says that doesn't help to ease her pain. Tilly dyes her tightly curled hair reddish-orange and always wears a signature black scarf. She wants to be a mortician because she feels that everyone deserves a proper send-off.

She smiles. "So how much trouble are you in?"

"None—this time. But Mrs. Washington warned me that next time, she'll call my parents. And if that happens, I'm pretty sure they'll murder me."

Tilly's eyes grow wide with unbridled enthusiasm. "How do you think they'll do it? Asphyxiation, drowning...Oh—cyanide in your milk?"

"What? No!" I shout.

She groans. "Oh, that's right, you don't drink milk."

"That really wasn't what I was objecting to," I reply.

"Well, remember you promised that—"

"I know, I know, Tilly. If I die before you, I'll leave paperwork behind stating you are the only one who can handle my body postmortem."

She hugs me and says, "Thank you!"

I roll my eyes and hug her back. "You know most best friends just do each other's hair and learn TikTok dances, right?"

She laughs. "Yeah, I know. So basic."

Tilly and I first met in the schoolyard in fourth grade. The boys were making fun of me, so I threw rocks at them and took off running. I ran smack into Tilly. We started hanging out from that day on. We'd sneak into my mom's room and put on her makeup. We looked like clowns. But in our minds, we were princesses who ruled a kingdom. It didn't take long for Tilly to add monsters to our land. So, naturally, I had to add a handsome hero to rescue us. Then Tilly discovered a weapon we could use to "defend" the land ourselves so we wouldn't need any heroes. What was this powerful weapon? A mascara wand. We called ourselves P3—Princess Protection Program. We saved a lot of pretend lives over the years.

Tilly still plays make-believe, but in a different way. She likes to collect cute, girly dollhouses and repurpose them into creepy homes Michael Myers would hesitate to walk into.

Although we're best friends, we don't always like the same things: I have a passion for sweet, sappy, and all-consuming romance books. Tilly loves romance, too, but the kind that comes from Edgar Allan Poe. One of Tilly's dreams is to be given a dozen black roses on Valentine's Day. My dream is to walk gracefully down fancy steps that lead to my true love. Is that too much to ask?

Apparently.

"I can't believe we've hit another Weeping Wednesday. Really, where does the time go?" Tilly says.

"Maybe this year, more people will get invites," I suggest, knowing full well how ridiculous I sound.

"What should we do this year to celebrate Casket Day?" Tilly asks.

One year after not getting an invite, we joked that our social lives had once again died. Tilly had said, *"Well then, we need to give them a proper send-off."* And that's how Casket Day started. Every year on Imani's birthday, we get casket-themed junk food, watch a retro rom-com movie (anything John Hughes), and take turns making up goofy ways our social life took its own life.

Last year, it took a tumble off the Empire State Building and landed flat on the sidewalk. The year before that, it took its last breath inside an industrial meat grinder. That was Tilly's year to make up the story.

"Aw, man!" I yell as I shut my locker door. "I forgot today's lunch was spicy nuggets and sweet potato fries. I should have followed Rahim tomorrow—meatball sub day. I hate meatball subs," I lament.

Tilly opens her locker, takes out a small foil pouch, and hands it to me: sweet potato fries and six nuggets.

Like I said, we're best friends.

Tilly and I live in the same area and usually walk home together. But today she tells me she's going in the opposite direction. "I'm sorry, Fancy. I'm working on a new miniature haunted house. And I need to get some more supplies."

A new house? Oh, that makes sense! In the past few weeks or so, she's been a little off. When I text her, she takes a while to get back to me. She doesn't return calls right away, and she hasn't come over lately. She's doing a new house! That explains everything.

I shrug. "Okay, I know better than to mess with your process. I can't wait to see it when it's done!"

CHAPTER 3

When I get home, I find a stack of mail on top of the desk near the door. One of the envelopes is from Mastercard. And from what I understand, Mastercard doesn't write to ask you how your week is going. Nope, it's a bill, and once my mom goes through it, she will know what I did. My heart starts beating faster with every passing moment. I hold the envelope in my hand and consider ripping it up so that there's no proof it ever existed. But I don't do that. I put the envelope back where I found it. I do that because of my strong morals and indestructible integrity (and also because I hear my mom's car pull up to the driveway).

I go to my room, close the door behind me, and address the framed image above my dresser. I'm not really sure when White Jesus and I became friends. But now that I think about it, it was inevitable. Like most Haitian homes, my house has half a dozen artistic depictions of Jesus. Some take the form of a poster, some are porcelain, and others are stitched on throw pillows. But no matter what form, Jesus is always there and *always* white.

My mom insisted I have a picture of White Jesus in my room, just like she does in her bedroom. I suggested maybe we should get a Black Jesus, since there's no way the real Jesus would have been white. My mom refused. "Never question" is kind of a theme in this house.

Over time, I started to slowly accept White Jesus. My views on His color didn't change, but it did occur to me that maybe we had something in common. Maybe White Jesus was a little stressed out by the pressure that came with living in a Haitian household.

That's why I'm turning to Him now. I'll need His help soon.

"Dear White Jesus, I know you and I haven't always been cool. I've questioned your judgment when it comes to certain things: mole rats, raisins, and the way you chose to put my body together. I look like a cubist painting! Would it have killed you to make my thighs, butt, and chest proportional?" I demand.

Fancy, is now really the time to go over old gripes?

"My point, WJ, is that I'm willing to overlook all the issues we have if you can get me out of this. Distract her in some way. I'm not advocating for a house fire or anything, but a small kitchen mishap?"

I hear my mom's footsteps getting closer; she's in front of my door now. "See, this is why you and I will always have issues!" I scold the poster.

American moms knock on their teenagers' doors and ask if they can come in; Haitian moms do not. And while my mother is a US citizen, trust and believe that Marie Augustine is very much a Haitian woman.

She barges in.

"Explain why you charged my credit card without asking me?" she says, her accent thickening more and more with every word. I look my mom over. She's a short, plump, light-skinned Black woman who could wither you with one glare.

"I didn't have a choice!"

"Falencia, your book budget is twenty-five dollars a month. That's it!"

"Mom, how am I supposed to live on that?"

"Back in Haiti, I had to stay home from school because the class trip was too expensive for our family. Do you know how much the trip was?"

Fifty cents.

"Fifty cents!" she says. "Your grandfather had ten kids, ten! We had to fetch the water from the well every day! Do you know how far the well was from our village?"

When she first told us about the well, it was three miles

from the village. But every time she tells the story, the well moves just a little farther away. One year it was ten miles from the village, and then thirteen.

"The well was twenty miles away!"

I want to roll my eyes, but Mom would snatch my eyeballs right from my head before I completed the gesture. The best thing to do is to let this story play out.

She goes on a rant about how the kids in Haiti work fourteen-hour days for pennies. How is it that I can't make twenty-five dollars work? There is no counterargument for that. Trust me, I've tried.

She ends her speech saying, "Do you know how many books you can buy for twenty-five dollars?"

I snort. "Yeah, e-books."

"E-books and paper books are the same thing!" she says, beside herself.

I groan loudly. "Can I pick up the soft, subtle scent of ink on the pages of an e-book? Or glide my fingertips along the shiny spine? No, I can't. Because e-books are not real books!"

"I gave you my card to take twenty-five dollars. But you took one hundred and fifty! I thought I could trust you."

I rush over to my bookshelf and pull out my purchase to show her. I hold up a pristine, sparkling gold-and-black box set.

"This is the Romance Lovers box set! The books have new covers, added material, and it's autographed! Look at it, Mom, isn't it pretty?" I ask, sliding my hand down the velvety finish of my new purchase. It gives me literal goose bumps.

She waves her hands in the air and looks toward the sky. "O bondye!" she says. That's Haitian Creole for "Oh my God." But more specifically, in this situation it means, "Oh my God, help me not to strike this child dead where she stands."

She comes over to me and slides the box set out of my hands before I can understand what's really happening.

"This is going with me," she announces.

"I just got those!" I shout.

"Nope, *I* just got those. You bought them with my money."

"You're going to return them?" I ask in complete dismay.

She places the books in front of her chest and hugs them tightly. Her lips curve into a wicked smile and her eyes glisten with malice.

"I could return these to the bookstore, but I won't. I'll display them up on the highest shelf in the house. It will be there for everyone to see—a shiny, pretty set of books that my daughter will never open!"

I plop down on my bed, in utter despair. How could she be so cruel? I think my mom missed out when she became a registered nurse. She has a talent for tormenting people. She'd be a real asset to the CIA.

A little while later, I hear Mom call out, "Fancy, bring your butt into the kitchen and help me get dinner on the table." I can tell by her tone that I better move fast.

Like in most Haitian kitchens, the windowsill has a row of glass coffee jars that have been repurposed and now hold various seasonings: anise, whole cloves, and bouillon cubes.

My mom tells me to fetch her the jar of epis out of the fridge.

Epis is the essential element to all Haitian cuisine. It's a thick blend of herbs, green peppers, garlic, and citrus juice. We could have a thousand dollars' worth of groceries, but if we are out of epis, then there is no food. Yup, it's that important.

I help her bring the food out to the dining room. She's made my favorites: fried snapper, plantains, and red beans and rice. It's not fair that her cooking is so good, especially when I'm trying to be mad at her. The delightful aroma of spices and seasonings fills the air and my stomach growls.

Shh! We're still mad at her!

My stomach doesn't get the memo. And clearly neither does my mouth, because it starts watering. If I were ever taken as a prisoner of war, I'd tell them everything they need to know for just one plate of red beans and rice. It's a good thing this country's national security doesn't depend on me.

We take a seat at the table just as my dad walks through the door. He's holding a small plastic bag and jumps when he sees Mom. He quickly puts the bag behind his back.

"Sweetheart! You're home! I thought you had choir rehearsal this evening," he says, laughing nervously as beads of perspiration appear on his forehead.

My mom and I are very active in our church. I wouldn't mind it so much except there are way too many services: I'm not sure why we bother to ask for forgiveness. We hardly get enough time to sin.

"Victor, I thought you were working late," she says as she gets up to greet him.

"It was a slow night, so I decided to come home early," Dad says uneasily. Dad is part owner of a cab company. He has to do a lot of admin stuff, but what he loves the most is driving—he's a people person.

Dad has a round tummy that spills out just beyond his belt and jiggles slightly when he laughs. He's a regular at the local flea markets and swap meets. My mom is not a fan and often makes him take the stuff back.

I think that's why Dad's eyes are darting around, making him look like a cat that wandered into a dog park. I'm guessing he just came from a flea market.

"The food smells so good. I'll be right back to have dinner with my beautiful wife and my lovely child," Dad says.

Yup, there's no doubt about it: Dad is hiding contraband.

"Victor, what is that behind your back?" Mom asks.

"Oh, it's nothing, sweetheart. Is that a new perfume you're wearing? It smells lovely," Dad says, trying to slowly make his way to the kitchen, where I suspect he will sneak out to the garage.

"I've been in the kitchen surrounded by fish grease. There is nothing lovely about that. Show me what you have behind your back."

He reluctantly shows her what he's been hiding: a white plastic bag that says REX FLEA MARKET.

"Victor!" Mom says.

He quickly takes out his newest purchase—a sorry-looking toaster, ready to be put out of its misery. He holds it against his chest like it's his baby.

"Sweetheart, this toaster is perfectly good," he insists.

"If it was perfectly good, why would someone throw it away?" Mom asks.

"Because Americans like to throw out perfectly good things. They have a whole season dedicated to it. They call it spring cleaning. But we know what it really is—American waste."

Mom's eyes narrow as she scans the item. "So the toaster works?"

He replies, "Yes—mostly. There are a few things missing— the bread lever, the browning-control knob, and one of the heating coils."

Mom laughs sardonically. "So the toaster is missing the parts that turn bread into toast?"

"Why must you always look at the negative? What about all the things this toaster *does* have?" Dad says.

Mom folds her arms across her chest. That's a sure sign Dad's losing the argument. So he wisely decides to pivot.

"You and Fancy have a hobby. You two listen to true-crime podcasts—for hours," he points out.

I jump up, unable to hold in my excitement. "Oh, Mom, I forgot to tell you—there's a new episode of *My Fair Murder*. It's about a dead grandmother who ran a gambling ring in the back room of a children's daycare. From the trailer, it sounds like it's one of her clients that did it. But she cheated on her husband, so he has a motive, too. And there's her shifty brother who hit her up for a major loan."

My mom leans in, eager for more info. "What did the body reveal?"

I smile, knowing this is the part she loves best. "The body was never found—until now!"

"Okay!" Mom says, beside herself. She loves when there's new evidence in an old case. That's when she lays out the best snacks. I know it's a little morbid, but you know who wholeheartedly approves of our hobby? Tilly. Naturally.

Dad's plan works. Soon, the two of us go down a true-crime rabbit hole and forget about his latest purchase.

After dinner, I go to my room and window-shop a new romance series I want to get. This is not the right time to beg Mom for the money, but I bookmark the series anyway.

I hear my mom call out for me. "Fancy, go get your dad's allergy pills at CVS before they close."

Oh no, not CVS....

CHAPTER
4

So, here's the thing about CVS Pharmacy—they kindly asked me to refrain from entering their establishment. That's a nice way of saying CVS has banned me. This happened last week, through no fault of my own. There I was, helping the New York economy by buying a pint of Chunky Monkey ice cream, when I walked by the magazine aisle, where one of the models on a cover was taunting me with a cruel laugh!

So I did what any normal girl would do—I yanked the magazine off the rack and ripped that judgy paper cover to shreds. It wasn't a big deal. I mean, it's almost 2025—who reads paper magazines anyway? The store manager took a slightly different view. She said to get out of her store and never come back. I'm not sure how serious she was about my never coming back, but when I think about entering the store, I picture being tackled by a gang of security guards. So I've been staying away. But now I have no choice.

I enter CVS and pull my hood over my head, keeping my eyes down. Hopefully, I can just walk in and get my dad's allergy pills without incident. I head down the aisle. I can feel the cashier's eyes on me as I enter. I know her; she was one of the many employees that saw my outburst. My heart is racing and my palms are sweaty. I remind myself that it's all in my head; they probably don't even remember me. There's no way they remember something that happened last week.

I see movement in the corner of my eye. The cashier I was afraid would recognize me walks out from behind her station. She's coming toward me, and I hope to White Jesus she's not coming to kick me out. Argh! Why didn't I just walk the extra four blocks to Rite Aid?

She walks up to me and then goes past me. She didn't even stop. She doesn't recognize me! Seriously, what was I so afraid of?

I take off my hood and browse the aisle like a normal person. A few moments later, I hear a rowdy crowd enter. I look up and see a group of guys from the basketball team—and among them is Rahim!

A bolt of lightning runs through me. I'm shaking and feverish. My eyes bulge out of my head; my whole body tingles with a mix of elation and utter fear. Yes, I'm freaking elated to be in the same space with him! But I'm also terrified to actually come face to face with him. He looks toward the aisle I'm in. I quickly squat down to the floor, so he won't see me.

I hear his unmistakably deep, melodic voice. He must have turned into one of the other aisles. I hear him and the other guys joking about something that happened at practice. I peek around the corner to see exactly where they are. They're milling around the back wall near the beverages and snacks. They clown around and grab armfuls of chips, dips, and enough candy to feed a small army.

Rahim calls out to one of the guys to pass him a party-size bag of Doritos—cool ranch flavor. That means he's got class. His teammate Tyson grabs it and throws it to him. The bag goes off course and lands right in front of me!

My first and only instinct is to run to the other aisle so that he doesn't see me. But then Mrs. Washington's words drift back to me....

"Fancy, why don't you just talk to him?"

Wait, why *don't* I just talk to him? I mean, it's one thing when we're in school; there's a hierarchy that must be obeyed. And people like me don't get to talk to people like Rahim. But here, in the sanctuary of aisle seven at CVS, all inequities have been abolished. This could be my chance to finally talk to the guy who takes up almost as much of my headspace as #BookTok.

"Where'd you throw it?" Rahim asks.

"I don't know, check over there. Or get another bag," Tyson says.

"Yo, for real? You're on the basketball team! Why you throw like my grandma?" Rahim replies.

"That's all you, man. I threw that thing right at you," Tyson counters.

"Whatever. Where is it?" Rahim asks again.

I look down at the bag of Doritos that is by my feet and suddenly a thought occurs to me. There must be a dozen CVS Pharmacies in this part of Brooklyn. What are the chances he'd come to the one right by my house? What's even more mind-blowing is that out of all the aisles for Tyson to hurl the snack, it lands in mine. C'mon! What are the odds? That's when it actually hits me—the thing that I have been missing this whole time, the thing that a romance reader would always, *always* detect.

Oh my gosh, could this be?

I'M IN A MEET-CUTE!

Okay, typically a meet-cute is when two strangers encounter each other for the first time in a funny, whimsical way. Rahim and I go to the same school, so we're not really strangers. Also, there's nothing inherently whimsical or romantic about aisle seven. Still, I think it counts.

"Tyson, for real? You can't throw a bag of chips? Why are you on the team?" he teases his friend.

"Again, not my fault you can't catch," Tyson replies.

Rahim groans and heads over to the aisle I'm in. I take a deep breath and steady myself—I can do this. This is my moment, my meet-cute! And just as Rahim approaches, I catch a glimpse of myself in the mirror on the sunglass display a few feet away. I look like hell! My hair is fuzzy; my coat is so puffy, it makes me look like I'm a float in the Macy's Thanksgiving Day Parade. And wait, is that a pimple? How the heck did I get a pimple between the time I left my house and now?

White Jesus, why do You hate me?

I can't do this. I can't talk to Rahim looking like a pre-filter selfie. I want to dash out the door, but there's just no time.

The moment he enters my aisle, I panic and grab the first thing on the shelf. I pretend to be looking at it. He doesn't notice me. I could have stayed there and everything would have been fine. But he's so close, panic gets the better of me. I drop the random box I grabbed and make a run for it. I go three aisles over to make sure there's enough space between us.

I lean on the nearby shelf for support. My legs are weak, there's a rush of white noise pounding in my ears, my face is flushed, and my heart is fluttering at speeds that might actually indicate oncoming heart troubles. I close my eyes and exhale.

Phew! At least I got away and nothing embarrassing happened!

"Hey, you dropped this," someone says.

My eyes pop open.

Rahim.

We are face to face. He hands me the box that I dropped. I hadn't paid attention to what it was. I pray it's not diarrhea medicine or something mortifying. I look down at the box, and that's when I see it....

Dear God, no!

I snatch the box from him and run out of the store. I don't stop running until I'm down the block. I think to myself that maybe I read the box wrong. There are hundreds of items in CVS; there's just no way I would randomly pick the worst possible item to have a guy catch me buying. But then I look down and there it is, in pink and white letters: VAGINAL ANTI-ITCH CREAM.

"ARGH!" I shout into the air.

Why me? Why, why, why?

It's hopeless; I'll never get a boyfriend! And even if I do by some miracle, there's no way in hell it will be Rahim. It turns out Casket Day is a real thing—I'm witnessing the actual death of my social life. It's a shame, because it was never really given a chance to live. I try to push back tears because crying will only make me look more pathetic.

I take out my cell to text the only person in the world who can make it better—Tilly. But this is just too much to text. I need to see her. I need a big hug badly. Whenever I freak out thinking I'll never get a boyfriend, she's always there to remind me that we don't need boys. She doesn't have a boyfriend, and yet she's happy. That can be me, too.

Tilly's house is only a few blocks from here, so instead of waiting for the bus, I walk over. I'm half a block from her house when I encounter a young couple passionately kissing. The jealousy I feel is palpable. I'm about to turn away when something about the girl catches my eye—a mess of bright-red curls....

"Tilly?"

I can't make sense of what I am seeing. All I know is I can't stay here. I bolt down the street and don't look back.

Who was the guy? How long have they been dating? How serious are they? Is he the reason she has been so distant lately? Is that why she is late returning my texts and sometimes takes days to call me back? How long has she been lying to me? Is she even making a new miniature house, or was that a lie, too?

By the time I got home, Tilly had called me several times, and each time I sent her to voicemail. I didn't want to hear anything she had to say. I went to bed early thinking I could escape, but I was wrong. I tossed and turned all night. The harder I tried to sleep, the more awake I became. I searched the furthest reaches of my mind to find a way to explain why Tilly would keep this secret from me. Finally, after hours of trying, my eyelids grew heavy and sleep found me. But when I wake up, I wake up to a revelation!

I text Tilly and we arrange to meet in the girls' locker room after gym.

I find her there pacing back and forth, looking super worried.

"Hi, Tilly."

She lets out a sigh of relief. "I thought you wouldn't talk to me ever again," she says, on the verge of tears. She moves in to hug me, and I hug her back. While we are still in each other's embrace, Tilly says, "I owe you an apology. I'm so sorry."

I hug her even tighter. "No, it's me. I am the one who should be sorry."

Tilly takes a step back. She looks puzzled. "What do you have to be sorry about?"

"Well, I was really upset when I saw you and that guy kissing. I ran home thinking my best friend had lied to me. I was destroyed. But when I woke up this morning, it all made sense."

"What do you mean?" she asks.

"You had no idea you were going to kiss that guy! This wasn't a story of a best friend being betrayed. This is a story about you finding yourself in a whirlwind romance that began only hours earlier! I can picture your meet-cute right now: You're at 7-Eleven, giving in to your need for a frozen treat. You head for the Slurpee machine. There's only one large cup left.

You both reach for it, and then—electricity courses through both of your fingers as you touch...."

"Ah, no. That's not what happened," she admits.

"Did a reckless cyclist zip by you, causing you to tumble into the street, and just as a car was about to run you over, a handsome guy stepped in and saved you? Is that how it happened?"

I am talking so fast that I don't let air into my lungs and start to feel a little lightheaded. I make myself take a beat.

Tilly looks at me with sad eyes.

"What is it?" I ask.

"The guy's name is Jason, and I didn't just meet him yesterday."

"Oh...so when did you meet him?" I ask as my heart starts pounding against my chest.

She looks off to the side, not wanting to face me. "We've been going out for two months. Fancy, he's my boyfriend."

"You've had a boyfriend for two months and you never told me? Why?"

"I know how important getting a boyfriend is to you, and I didn't want you to be mad at me for getting one first. And plus, you...you're not really good with change. I mean, you're actually spectacularly bad with change."

My mouth drops open and my whole body tenses up. "I am not bad with change. I can handle change!"

"Fancy, last week I got banana frozen yogurt instead of my usual cookies and cream, and you freaked out."

"No rational person would go from cookies and cream to banana. So I inquired about a possible health issue."

"You asked me if I was having a brain aneurysm!"

"Well, excuse me for caring about your health!" I snap.

"And remember the homeless lady by our school? The one who sings the same song every day as we pass by her? Then one day she changed her song, and you wouldn't leave her alone until she went back to the original."

"'Single Ladies' is an American classic! But I guess it doesn't ring a bell for you because you aren't single! You have a boyfriend! One you've had for eight weeks and never told me about!"

"Fancy, I'm sorry."

I wipe my eyes with the back of my hand. "Whatever, Tilly. I don't care," I lie.

Tilly looks over my shoulder and her jaw drops. Something behind me is causing her eyes to pop out of her head. The look of dread on her face forces me to turn around and see what she's looking at. I turn and come face to face with the worst possible person to have overheard our argument— Cheer! She clears her throat and says, "Sorry, I was looking for my— Oh, there it is." She picks up her cell phone, which was lying on a nearby bench. She tries to conceal her devious smirk, but it's written all over her; she is enjoying the piping-hot gossip she just overheard. And before we can say anything to explain what's going on, Cheer runs out of the locker room.

I groan and nod to myself. "Yeah, this is just perfect."

"It sucks that you found out this way. I'm sorry. You and I are still best friends. We can figure it out," Tilly vows.

I look at her with a mix of anger and bitterness. "Best friends? I don't think you even know what that means," I say as I turn and walk away.

CHAPTER 5

Mrs. Washington opens the door to her office and finds me lying on the floor, my arm draped over my eyes.

"Fancy, what are you doing here? I almost stepped on you. And how did you get in here? My door was locked."

"I'm not in trouble," I promise her.

"You broke in, so I wouldn't be too quick to make that statement if I were you."

"Henry the janitor let me in. I told him I forgot my stuff in here."

"He shouldn't have let you in just like that."

"It's not his fault. I have a very trustworthy face."

"Don't do that again. Now, if you're not in trouble, what are you doing here?"

"Bemoaning my outcast state," I say.

"Girl, it's been a long day—too long for Shakespeare and hysterics. Get up from the floor. What is it? Did Rahim get a bodyguard?"

"Wow, you've got jokes. Respect," I reply as I gather myself and slump into the nearby chair.

"Fancy, did you move things around on my desk?" she says.

"Yes. They were askew; I'd like to respectfully request that we don't make any changes to your desk. I find it...unsettling."

"You do know it's my desk, right?" she reminds me.

"As you pointed out, I come here rather often. So I like to think of it as ours. Also, you changed your hand sanitizer from white tea pear to lavender coconut. Is that a temporary change, or..."

She purses her lips. "Fancy, why are you here? Talk fast."

I tell her everything that happened last night and this morning with Tilly, as well as the CVS catastrophe and being overheard by Cheer.

I can tell by the sympathetic look on Mrs. Washington's face that things really are as bad as I thought. She reluctantly asks a follow-up question about CVS. "The box you took off the shelf, was it—"

"Maximum strength? Yeah, it was." I groan and bury my face in my hands.

"Oh, Fancy, I'm sorry. And I can't imagine how hard it was to have to stop and pay for it."

"Pay? I just ran out of there. I wasn't thinking. Great, now I'm a criminal," I say, mostly to myself. "Well, if I wasn't banned from CVS before, I sure am now."

"On the bright side, there's a good chance that Rahim wasn't even paying attention to the box you dropped. Most likely, he has no idea what it was."

"That would be great, but I doubt it. Anyway, I can handle that—mostly. What about Tilly and her betrayal? How do I deal with that?"

"I know you're hurt that she lied to you, but Tilly sounds like she's really sorry," Mrs. Washington says.

"It's not just that, Mrs. Washington—she has a boyfriend now. *Everything* is going to change."

She groans. "And we all know how you feel about change."

"Exactly! Remember the frozen—"

"Frozen yogurt incident. We had a double session that day."

I sigh deeply. "It's all over. Seven years of friendship, gone. Just like that!"

"Why can't you be friends even though she has a boyfriend?"

I look at her earnestly. "I never thought I'd use this Haitian expression, but here goes: Rocks in the river will never know the pain of rocks in the sun."

She purses her lips together to keep from laughing. "So you're the rock in the sun?"

"Yes! Tilly was in the sun with me. We were two unpopular girls who had nothing but each other; yet, because of that, we had everything. But now, Tilly is in a river, splashing around, having a good time. She won't remember life in the blazing sun. She won't remember me."

"I think you're jumping to conclusions. Your friendship can handle this. Give her some credit," Mrs. Washington says.

"She's gone to the other side and left me. It's just me now. Alone." I sigh and look out the window.

"You are the most dramatic teenager at Ellen Craft High. Now listen to me," she says in a firm voice. "Just because Tilly has a boyfriend doesn't mean she can't make room for you. Yes, things will be different—slightly. But the important things will be the same. You two will still be close and still have each other's backs."

I don't know I'm crying until I feel the warm tears slide down my cheek. Mrs. Washington hands me a box of tissues. I take one and wipe my tears.

"Two-ply. I'm honored."

"Falencia, I promise you, everything is going to be okay."

I look away from her and toward the window. I don't want her to see more tears. She puts a hand on my shoulder. I speak, but my voice sounds far away. "My parents put me in ballet when I was a kid. No matter what I tried, that first class I just couldn't find my balance. It was the same way at school. Every day I would wake up and hope that just this once, I could stay upright and not fall flat on my face.

"The next time we had class, my teacher showed me how to keep my balance. She taught me how to pick a point on the wall and focus on it. And no matter how fast the room spun or how difficult the turn was, I never fell down so long as I had a focus point. That's Tilly—she's my focus point. She's the reason I don't fall down at school."

"Fancy, nothing about your friendship will change. I promise you, Tilly is the very same person she always was."

I'm not sure if Mrs. Washington is right or not, but either way, I can't stay in her office forever. I have to go and find out. I thank her for her time and the use of her high-end tissues.

I walk out the door toward my locker. A few yards away from me, I see Tilly trip and drop the stack of papers and folders she was holding. I run over to her.

"I can help," I say as I kneel beside her.

"No, no, it's okay. I got it," she says in a panicky voice.

"Tilly, it's fine. I know things are weird between us, but I want to help."

She smiles sadly, and we quickly gather her stuff. "Thanks," she says softly.

Something in the corner catches my eye—a blue folder. It slid over by the lockers. "We missed one. I got it," I say as I bend down to retrieve it. I accidentally hold the folder upside down and everything falls out. Among the mess is a bright red envelope with gold engraving.

Tilly has an invite to Imani's party.

My focus point is well and truly gone.

I'm falling down….

I pick up the envelope; it feels smooth between my fingers, like the blade of a dagger.

"Is this an invite to Imani's party?" I ask, although the answer is obvious.

"Yeah, she handed it to me in class last period," she says.

I would like to tell myself that things will be okay, but I know better. In a few weeks Tilly will go through those double doors to Imani's house, and then she'll never look back. She'll forget about me.

The two of us stand there, in the middle of the hallway, our eyes fixed on each other. The students whiz past us, but we stay motionless, stuck in this moment. That's when it hits me—I can't believe it took me so long.

"ARGH! Imani is so freaking devious!" I shout.

"What?"

I take Tilly's hand in mine and fill her in. "Yesterday, Imani was pissed because I said I had true friends. She was all in her feelings about it. So, I'm sure once Cheer told her about our argument, she saw her chance to stick it to me. She gave you an invite because she's trying to get back at me. She doesn't want you at her party; she's just using you to get at me."

"Why would you say that?"

"I'm just telling you what Imani is thinking."

"How do you know what she's thinking? Maybe she just wants to get to know me," Tilly says, sounding hurt.

"Oh, c'mon, since when?"

"Are you saying I'm not worth getting to know?"

"I'm saying Imani never did anything that didn't benefit her. She saw a way to get back at me, and so she gave you the invite."

"You're unbelievable. Why can't you just be happy for me?"

"What? Wait—you're not falling for this, are you, Tilly? C'mon, don't be stupid!"

"Oh, so now I'm not only the girl who can't get an invite of her own, I'm stupid, too? You are unbelievable, Falencia Augustine!" Tilly snaps. And before I can reply, she storms off down the hall.

CHAPTER 6

"How's my favorite child?" my mom says sweetly as she walks into the kitchen. She comes close and tucks a stray braid behind my ear.

"I'm your only child," I remind her. "And, I'm fine. What's up?" I ask.

"Well, the church is doing a clothing drive. Some of the older ladies need help sorting the clothes. I signed up to help one of them, but I have to go back to the hospital and cover a shift. Can you go instead of me? Please, my favorite daughter?"

I sigh. "Okay, Mom. I'll do it."

"You said yes way too easily. What's wrong?"

I'd like to tell my mom what's up with Tilly and me, but once I use the word *boyfriend*, she will lose it. Haitian families don't allow their daughters to date or to associate with a girl who is dating. So I ignore my urge to spill my guts, and assure my mom that I really do want to help out. I figure it might keep my mind off Tilly and her boyfriend.

A half hour later, I'm standing in front of Ms. Dorcy's apartment. There's a sticker on it that reads, I HAVE MONEY, I JUST WON'T BUY FROM YOU. Wow. I guess they were out of plain old NO SOLICITING signs. I knock on the door, and she opens it, looking like she's about to bark at me for knocking.

Ms. Dorcy is in her early seventies, but her skin could pass for early sixties very easily. She used to be a piano teacher. It's a natural fit, given her long, graceful fingers.

In church, the kids have a theory that the reason she looks so young is because she feasts on the blood of innocent children. I'm not saying I agree with them. I did, however, turn on the Find Me app on my cell, allowing local authorities to triangulate my location, should I suddenly disappear.

She looks me up and down and comes to a conclusion. She thinks I'm suspect.

"I'm here to help you with the clothes," I say.

"I know you from church. The one with the silly name."

"Okay, sure," I reply, ready to get this over with.

I walk inside her apartment. If the universe had a junk drawer, this apartment would be it. There are so many knickknacks and oddities, it's overwhelming. On the plus side, the house is warm and feels nice after the chill of being outside. She takes me to her living room, which has a grand piano in the corner.

"So, where's the bag you want me to help you sort?"

"A bag? Ha! Try three," she says, moving so I can see the three large black trash bags in the middle of the living room.

Oh, you have got to be kidding me!

"Now, I suppose you'll be wanting something to drink?" she asks. There's nothing about her tone that indicates she's actually offering me a drink. It's more like an observation— she's observing that normal, non-awful people would offer someone a drink in this case.

"No, it's okay. I'm fine. Thank you."

"Yeah, well, too late. I already poured it." She goes into the kitchen and comes back with a green-colored hammered drinking glass. It's filled halfway with a dark liquid.

"Um, what is it?" I ask.

"Coke."

I look at the glass and reply, "I think it might be flat."

"Yes, for about a week now. But I'm not throwing out a perfectly good bottle of soda just because there are no more bubbles. Drink up."

"Maybe later," I reply, placing the glass on the coffee table in the center of the living room.

We set up a system where she points to which pile she wants

things to go in. There's one pile for her relatives and one for the church. She plays some classical music in the background as we work. We're just starting to get into some type of rhythm when I get a text from Tilly.

TILLY: We really need to talk!

ME: Why? Are there more boyfriends you neglected to tell me about?

I type furiously. Ms. Dorcy watches me and says, "Who's getting on your nerves so much you have to make that face?"

"It's nothing, just my best friend, Tilly. At least, I think she's still my best friend. I don't even know anymore," I admit.

"Well, we have nothing but time. Start talking," she says as we continue to sort the clothes.

"I don't really want to talk about it." One look at Ms. Dorcy, though, tells me she wasn't making a request, so I start talking. I plan to just give her the Twitter-length short version, but soon I'm laying out the whole story. I think the reason I'm comfortable being so open is that, for all her faults, Ms. Dorcy is a very good listener.

When I'm done telling her everything, I expect her to caution me about losing friends. I also expect her to give me the "You're being too dramatic" talk, like most adults would. I'm wrong on both counts. When I'm done, she nods and simply says, "Good for you!"

I'm taken aback to say the least. "Wait, you don't think I'm overreacting?" I ask.

"Heck no! She was your best friend and she betrayed you. Now you have to cut her out of your life, without mercy."

I try to process what she's saying. She stops working and adds, "You know what, I think I got some of the good stuff in the back of the fridge. I'm gonna get it. And when I come back, I'll tell you a story about my supposed best friend and how it all went wrong."

"Wow, okay..."

She goes away and comes back with two mini cans of Diet Coke. She hands me one and takes the other for herself. I pop it open. This one still has bubbles. I feel loved—or Ms. Dorcy's version of love. She begins her tale.

"I once had a best friend. Her name was Clara. We were roommates in music school. We were the best of friends, until she betrayed me!"

I ask my follow-up question carefully, not wanting to overstep. "Can I ask what she did?"

She stops sorting and looks out into the distance as if the story is playing out in her head and she's doing the narration. "Well, it happened Thanksgiving night. She came over, and we had us a good time and a great meal. I put some leftovers for her in my best Tupperware. Then a week later, I call and tell her it's time to bring my bowls back, and do you know what she said? She said she couldn't remember where she put them and that she'd let me know when she found them. *When* she found them! Can you believe the nerve of that woman? Well, ever since then, I've wiped my hands clean of her."

"Wait—I don't get it. When did she betray you?" I ask, certain I've missed something.

"Didn't you hear what I said? She took my Tupperware—my good Tupperware!"

"You stopped being best friends just for that?"

"Yes, that was enough. Once someone lies and betrays you, there's no way back."

"Don't you miss her?" I ask.

"Oh, that fades. Soon that hole in your heart will be cured by the best medicine of all: indifference."

She opens her mini can of Diet Coke and sips. Meanwhile, I'm having trouble keeping the liquid down. It's swooshing around in my belly. The thought of not talking to Tilly for years and years makes me nauseated.

"So you never tried to find another best friend? You're all alone?" I ask.

"Oh no! I have a very good friend, Charlie. He has never let me down. He's always here for me when I need him."

I feel relief seep into my body and the queasy feeling is gone. So there is life after the ending of a strong friendship? Thank goodness.

"Well, I'm glad you have Charlie. Have I seen him before? Does he come to the church?"

She laughs. "Why would I bring him there?"

"Oh. Okay. Maybe I'll meet him someday."

"Why wait?" She takes something from the coffee table and hands it to me. "Say hi to Charlie."

She hands me her TV remote control.

The thought that Tilly and I could end up like Ms. Dorcy and her former best friend terrifies me. So I text Tilly, and we agree to meet for pizza tomorrow.

Now as we sit across from each other in our favorite booth, I'm wondering if this was a good idea. There's nothing but silence between us.

Tilly and I have never had an issue starting up a conversation or keeping it going. If anything, we spend all night on the phone and then wonder why we're so sleepy the next day. We've actually both fallen asleep on the phone, midsentence. According to my dad, if Tilly and I had been born in the early days of cell service, when companies made people pay extra for going over their allotted minutes, we'd have bankrupted both of our families.

But looking at us right now, you'd never know that we are close, let alone best friends.

We each have a slice of pizza in front of us. Per usual, Tilly has chosen to top hers with extra cheese. And on the table, alongside the pizza, she has gathered a handful of mustard packets. Soon she'll dump the mustard over the pizza and swear it's delicious. We've been having the "mustard on pizza" debate since we were kids. She says it adds a zing to it. I think it's sacrilege to spoil a slice of Original Ray's Pizza with a topping so clearly meant for a hot dog or a pretzel. But I'm used to it by now. And seeing her neatly stacked pouches of mustard standing by ready to ruin a perfectly good pizza—well, it feels familiar and oddly comforting.

The food remains uneaten, though, and neither of us makes a move to change that. We play with the tips of our straws by twirling them between our fingers.

We both start speaking at the same time, saying each other's names. I signal to Tilly that she can speak first.

"I'm really sorry I didn't tell you about Jason. I know how much you hate change, and, well, I wasn't sure you could handle it—but I was wrong. Handle it or not, I should have told you."

I shrug. "Well, to be fair, it has been pointed out to me that I may have an issue with change. And maybe telling me about such a big one was hard."

"It really was. But that's in the past. Jason and I were talking, and we'd love to hang out Tuesday, just the three of us."

We? When did they become we?

"Um, yeah, sure," I reply, refusing to overthink the "we" part of the conversation. "So, what about Imani's party? Are you going?"

"Nah. You're probably right. She only invited me because she was trying to get to you. Why would she want me at her party?" Tilly says, crestfallen.

"Tilly, you're a badass! It's about time that Imani and the whole world sees that. If you want to go to that party, then go! They're lucky to have you."

Her expression softens and she replies, "Thanks!"

I nod and study her face. "So, are you going?"

She gives me a little smile and says, "Nah. I'd rather hang with you and have a kickass Casket Day!"

"Perfect!"

"So...you want to hear more about Jason, or is it too soon?" she asks carefully.

I laugh. "Yes, I want to hear all about him. And after that, I'll tell you about me running into Rahim at CVS..."

"What happened?" she asks. I tell her everything. She looks at me with sympathy but can't hide a small smile.

"I know, it was awful. I don't want to even think about it. Now tell me everything about Jason. Spill it!"

She tells me that they met at the craft store when he went to pick up something for his grandma. She said their hands touched while reaching for the same box of Popsicle sticks. Tilly says she felt the hairs on the back of her neck stand up and had goose bumps running up and down her arms. She gazed into his searing steely gray eyes and couldn't look away.

He smells like wintergreen spearmint gum, mixed with his dad's woodsy aftershave. His hands feel like black velvet on her skin, his laughter could be used as currency, and once in a while he calls her "babe." In short, Jason is perfect.

"And don't worry, Fancy, I remembered everything you told

me about a first kiss: make sure you're near a fan, so that way your hair can blow in the wind, Beyoncé style. And if you're outside, stand in the windiest spot and gently shake your head just before he kisses you."

"Good girl!" I reply. We laugh and it feels just like old times. My shoulders relax, and all the butterflies in my stomach are gone. When it's time to go, I help Tilly clear the table and notice that the stack of mustard packets remains unopened.

"Hey, no mustard topping?" I ask.

She shrugs. "I don't know. Guess I'm evolving."

That's when I feel it—a slight flutter. Maybe there's one stray butterfly left....

CHAPTER
7

On my way home, I got an email from Mrs. Washington.
She referred to the story I told her about Jean-Louis, the boy
who was sent back to Haiti. She found a way to weaponize my
folksy tale and use it against me. She compiled a list of assignments I owe all my teachers, including Mr. Doyle. She sent it
to me in an email titled, "Jean-Louis Playlist." And at the bottom of the email is a link to a Spotify playlist, featuring twenty
songs about time running out. I couldn't really be mad at her; I
have a soft spot for musically themed passive aggression.

In the morning, I stop by her office and update her on Tilly
and me. She in turn makes me promise yet again to focus on

my schoolwork. I plan to do just that—after I hang out with Tilly and Jason. Before I leave her office, though, I confess to Mrs. Washington that there's another reason why I stopped by.

"Oh, and what reason would that be?" she asks.

"To drop off a small gift." I take a seat across from her and place a package on her desk. It's a gift-wrapped box the size of an iPhone. The red bow I picked out is perfectly centered.

"This is very sweet, Fancy, but you didn't have to get me anything. I held back on calling your parents because I know you've had a tough time lately. But if you don't finish the list of assignments, I'll have to call them," she warns.

"I know, and this gift is not about that—well, it's not *just* about that. Do you remember the last time I was here? You changed from your usual sanitizer, and I didn't argue with your decision."

She suppresses a smile. "Thank you for your support."

"You're welcome. But now, I think we can both agree, it's time for your harrowing experiment to end. You need to go back to white tea pear."

She eyes the box with growing suspicion. "Did you get me…?"

I smile but don't say anything. She opens the gift.

"White tea pear hand sanitizer. What are the odds?" she says. She folds her arms over her chest. "Fancy, I thought you were more open to change. Hence hanging out with Tilly and Jason tomorrow."

"That's exactly my point. I'm letting Jason into my little circle with Tilly. That's a humongous change. Surely you won't force me to endure even more change so quickly. I'm just one person."

She takes the bottle of sanitizer and replaces the new one on her desk.

"Fancy...," she begins, after taking a pregnant pause.

"Yes?"

"I just want to make sure you manage your expectations. Some things won't be exactly the same as they were before. Give it a chance. Be open to new things."

"Yeah, I got it. Try new things or lose my one and only friend. Copy that!" I reply, hoping to pull off a casual tone.

Tonight is my very first "official" meeting with Tilly's boyfriend. We've decided to go to a movie and get some food after. My mom has choir rehearsal all this week and won't be home until late. That works out great, because if she were here, she'd have a million questions about where I'm going and why. Well, if today is anything to go by, she doesn't need to worry—I'll never get a boyfriend.

I already suspected that to be the case, but I received confirmation this morning when I saw Rahim in the middle of a crowd of kids, making his way around the corner. I thought maybe Mrs. Washington was right and he didn't even see the box at CVS.

So I put it out of my mind and followed him. And when he

stopped suddenly, I bumped right into him. Well, this was my chance. Tilly had tried something new, and now I should, too, right? All I had to do was say something to him—anything.

But Rahim beat me to the punch and started the conversation. "Hey, aren't you that girl that—"

Before he could finish the question, I found myself fleeing down the hall.

"He was right there. Why didn't I say something?" I shout to White Jesus, as if He could reply. The flashback of running into Rahim at school makes me shiver with embarrassment.

I take a deep breath and regroup. Once I'm done getting dressed, I look myself over in the mirror. I'm dressed in ankle boots, jeans, and a V-neck sweater. It's one of these rare days where I think, *Hey, I'm actually kind of cute*. I don't have a lot of those, so yeah, I linger a little longer than I need to.

One of the reasons I'm having an "I'm cute" moment is because my boobs are also having a moment. They're perky-adjacent and happy tonight. Tomorrow, I can put on the same outfit, wearing the same bra, and I won't look nearly this good. It's a truth universally accepted by us girls: boobs have a mind of their own and won't be dictated to.

I wonder about the girls who walk around looking and feeling good all the time. What must that be like? I'm thinking that when they walk out their doors, a rainbow appears in the sky and carries them to whatever destination they desire. Like some kind of elite transportation system for the beautiful people.

I've watched Imani in the halls in the past few days, and

she's even more popular than ever. So remember that feeling of "I'm cute"? Well, that's gone. I'm looking into the same mirror, but its opinion of me has changed.

"Hey, show me looking cute like you did a few minutes ago or I'm throwing you into the black abyss that all mirrors fear: the back of the closet!"

The mirror doesn't cooperate.

I turn to White Jesus. "What about You—do You think I look good tonight?"

I could swear White Jesus parts His lips and says, *Meh.*

"Wow, really, WJ?"

Well, cute or not, if I don't leave the house right now, I'll be late to meet Tilly and Jason.

Tilly and Jason.

Still not used to that.

I pin my braids back, spray on some perfume, and apply a light coat of gloss with a slight reddish undertone. It's a classic Rihanna-approved gloss, but I'm pretty sure when I step out of the house, no rainbow will appear.

Oh well . . .

I look at the mirror once more. And I'm back to kind of cute again.

I step into the hall and make my way down the stairs quietly. My mom isn't here, but still, it's best that I not be seen. I don't want to broadcast the fact that I'm going out on a school night. As luck would have it, I'm not the only one taking advantage of the fact that Mom's not here.

I'm halfway down the stairs when I catch my dad red-handed coming out of the kitchen. He's carrying a roasted turkey leg and his latest ill-advised flea market purchase. This time it's a countertop blender. The blender has a dull chrome surface, missing buttons, and a frayed cord.

We make eye contact, and Dad says, "This is not what you think. I did not go to the flea market."

I reply, "While you weren't at the flea market, I was not hanging out with Tilly on a school night."

"And what time will you be back from the place you didn't go to?"

"Eleven."

"Try again."

"Okay, ten thirty."

"I expect to see you in your room by nine."

"Okay, okay. Back at nine."

We nod, trusting each other to keep quiet. What can I say? Mutually assured destruction is a beautiful thing.

We meet up at the AMC movie theater downtown. It's early, so the theater isn't crowded, but it's still fairly busy for a weeknight. Tilly and Jason come through the doors together.

"Fancy, this is my boyfriend, Jason. Jason, this is my best friend, Fancy."

It's the very first time I'm getting a really good look at

Jason. He's tall, slender, and on the pale side. Everything about Jason screams quintessential Bohemian hippie: his earth-toned fedora, oversized fringe scarf, and beaded necklace. Tilly looks on as we greet each other. She tells me that Jason isn't normally into horror movies, but that he's coming tonight just for her.

"Oh, really, horror isn't your thing? Then what kind of movies do you like?" I ask.

"I don't usually vibe with movies. I find them lacking in human connection."

Okay...

Tilly quickly chimes in. "Jason is really into different vibes and also frequencies."

"It's true. Everything around us has its own frequency. Like this theater—it's vibrating and doing its own thing. Do you hear it, Fancy?" he asks.

"Nope," I reply flatly.

Jason looks me over and nods with newfound understanding. "No wonder you can't hear it. Your energy's blocked. When was the last time you checked your chakra?"

"You know, it's been a while," I reply, pressing my lips together so I don't laugh. Tilly shoots me a look. "We better get some snacks; the movie is gonna start soon."

Jason excuses himself to go to the restroom while we go to the snack bar. The moment he's out of earshot, Tilly grabs my arms and asks me what I think of Jason.

"I'm sorry, it's hard to think," I confess.

"Why?"

"Because you're stopping the blood flow from getting to my brain."

Tilly looks down and realizes she has an iron grip on my upper arms. She blushes and says, "Oh, sorry."

"It's okay, and yes, he's very cute. And I don't know him well enough to say if he's smart, but he picked you, so I'm guessing he's very smart," I reply.

She gives me a big hug. When I hold her close, I can feel her heart pounding against her chest.

"Tilly, relax. He's chill and so am I. There's no need to be anxious."

She takes a deep breath, and I advise her to take a few more. She follows my suggestion, and I can see her shoulders relaxing.

A few minutes later, junk food in hand, we take our seats inside the theater. We're seeing *The Haunting in Connecticut*. It came out, like, a million years ago, but it's one of our favorites, especially around Halloween.

Normally Tilly isn't scared of horror movies. But there's this one part in this film when the girl turns on the light in her bedroom and the evil spirit leaps out, ready to eat her face. We don't know why, but that part gets to Tilly. She always puts one hand over her mouth so she doesn't scream, and grabs mine with the other one. She's been known to leave a mark.

We're more than halfway through the movie when the part Tilly fears comes on. I brace myself for the feeling of my hand being lovingly crushed by my bestie. On the screen, the girl opens her bedroom door....

This is it. Hand-crushing time.

But I don't feel Tilly's hand squeezing mine. Instead, she's grabbed Jason's. It's not that she's no longer scared; it's that she no longer needs comfort from me. She has a boyfriend now....

Okay, Jason, you can have the hand squeeze.

After, we make our way across the street to the burger place. It's an old-fashioned diner with bright red booths and mini jukeboxes on each table. We pile into the booth farthest from the door, so we can avoid the gust of cold air that follows when a customer comes in or out.

Tilly and I usually order double cheeseburgers and split a huge plate of chili cheese fries. We wash that down with Diet Cokes and a brownie à la mode. It usually takes mere seconds for us to order because we always get the same thing. This time, however...

"I don't know, Jay. What do you think I should get?" she asks.

Since when does Tilly need help picking out what to eat?

"Get the double cheeseburger. You always get the double cheeseburger," I remind her.

She smiles brightly. "Yeah, they make a good one here."

Jason gives her a dubious look. "A burger, babe? Is that *really* what we want?"

We? Are they gonna be alternating bites?

65

"Well..." She looks down at the menu and then at Jason.

He shrugs. "You get whatever you want, babe."

I have never rolled my eyes so hard in my entire life. I think I might have actually injured myself. Is this guy for real?

"I was kind of getting tired of red meat anyway. I'll have the chick—" Jason clears his throat. "I mean, the veggie burger," Tilly says.

"That sounds great, babe." He smiles, and she melts.

Ugh. I'd trade places with the cow right now.

"Great, I'll have the same," he says. After we place our orders, Jason turns his attention to me.

"So, you two are good friends—" he says.

"Best friends," I correct him. Tilly and I exchange a warm look.

"That's why I'm so confused," Jason adds.

"Confused about what?" I ask.

"Imani's party," he replies. Tilly flashes him a warning. He takes her hand and says, "Babe, holding back what you feel can really affect your aura. Besides, best friends should communicate. I bet we can clear up everything, but only if you tell Fancy how you really feel."

I turn to her; she starts flipping the music selection cards on the mini jukebox at the table.

"Tilly, what's he talking about?"

"It's nothing," she replies.

"You couldn't talk about anything else but this party," Jason says. "You even bought a dress the same day you got the invite."

My head is spinning. "You bought a dress?"

"That was before we met up for pizza and talked...," Tilly explains.

"I asked you if you wanted to go, and you said no," I reply.

"Of course I said no. I didn't want to hurt your feelings. You looked crushed at even the thought of me going. I couldn't do that to you."

I'm shivering, and the door to the diner has not been opened. The chill is coming from inside me. I don't know what to say. Does she think I'm so pathetic that I would fall apart if she were to go to the party?

"Well, I didn't want to tell you this because I thought you didn't want to go, but now that I know that you do, I can share the news with you. Imani invited me to her party!"

CHAPTER
8

I'm not sure what response I was expecting to my announcement. And the truth is, I wasn't even sure what I was announcing until the words came out of my mouth. But now that it's out there, it's only right that Tilly and Jason react. And yet, both just stare back at me with blank expressions.

"What? Why are you guys not saying anything?" I ask as I casually put a fry in my mouth. It tastes like wood, and the more I chew it, the harder it seems to get. I force myself to swallow and go on as if everything is fine.

Nope, nothing to see here, people. It's just Fancy Augustine telling the biggest lie of her life....

"You got invited to Imani's party?" Tilly asks.

"Yeah. That's what I said," I reply, avoiding eye contact.

Tilly and Jason exchange a look. I'm not sure what the look means, but I don't think it's good.

"When did this happen?" she says.

"Just before I got ready to come hang out. She came by my house and...delivered it personally."

Tilly and Jason exchange a look of doubt.

"Why do I feel like you don't believe me?" I ask, genuinely starting to take offense.

"It's just...I feel like getting an invite to Imani's party is something you would have told me right away."

"I guess I needed time to process."

Tilly nods. We start eating silently. I make circles in a glop of ketchup using a French fry. I'm hoping that it somehow comes off as an "I'm totally confident" vibe.

She looks like she's about to say something but then thinks better of it. She does this twice, and finally I can't take it any longer.

"Tilly, just say what's on your mind!" I say.

"It just seems...unlikely that you'd hold back such a big piece of news, that's all," Tilly says.

I could let it go. I *should* let it go, but I don't. "It seemed unlikely that you'd hide Jason from me, but you did."

She bites her lip and looks off to the side.

"I'm gonna go get some more napkins. I'll be right back," Jason says.

"Stay," Tilly requests. She looks me in the eye and says, "Yes, I lied to you about something that was important. I was wrong. I admitted that. You said you forgave me."

"I did. Doesn't mean I forgot."

She nods and laughs sardonically. "So that's what this is? You're getting back at me for lying, by lying?"

My jaw drops. I fold my arms over my chest as heat floods my cheeks. "You're calling me a liar? That's it. Good day to you, madam!"

"What—"

"I said, good day!"

For the record, I have no idea why I ended the conversation like I was in a Jane Austen novel. But it felt right and I was already committed, so I doubled down.

The next morning, I seek refuge in Mrs. Washington's office. I tell her everything that happened, and I make it quick before the first bell rings.

"Can you believe she accused me of lying?" I ask her.

"But you are lying!" she points out.

I shrug. "If you want to be technical."

She opens her drawer and takes out a small bottle of aspirin.

"You would be proud to know, when I got home from the fiasco that was dinner, I calmly went over my options."

"Calmly?" she says, dubious.

"Okay, I cried to White Jesus, slumped down on my bed, and ate a whole pint of ice cream."

She follows up with genuine curiosity. "And what part of that would I be proud of you for?"

"The ice cream—it was rocky road. So even at my lowest, I adhere to symbolism."

She holds up her index fingers, signaling for me to hold on. She takes two pills and downs them with the bottle of water on her desk. Once she's done, I continue.

"After the pint of symbolism, it suddenly hit me. All I have to do is be super nice to Imani, and soon my natural charm will win her over. Then she'll gladly invite me to her party."

"Or you could be honest with Tilly. Tilly, remember her? Your best friend?" she says pointedly.

"You didn't see the pathetic look she gave me. I have to show her, Imani, and the whole school that I am not a loser!"

"Tilly doesn't think that about you. Have you ever thought that maybe you're projecting your thoughts onto her?"

I think for a beat. "Nope."

Mrs. Washington hangs her head in frustration. Then she asks, "How is your to-do list going? Are you getting any homework done?"

"I know I owe a few—" I start.

"Many. Fancy, you owe *many* assignments. And remember this is your last chance with me. Got it?"

"Copy that."

She comes around the desk and sits in the chair right next to me. "And Fancy, it's just a party."

And that's when I see Mrs. Washington for the first time; I mean, I *really* see her. And not just who she is right now, but who she used to be. I see her at fifteen—thin, pretty, and confident. She's the girl in class everyone adores. She has smooth skin, an easy smile, and she puts distinctly feminine, curly loops at the ends of her letters. She has plenty of friends, dates, and party invites.

"Never mind. I don't think you understand. Curly-loop-type girls rarely do."

"Curly loop? What loops?" she asks.

Before I can reply, the first bell rings. "I gotta go. See you later."

She shouts after me, "Fancy, do your homework! And that's not a suggestion!"

I walk to my locker, hoping I can get my stuff before Tilly gets here. But just as I pull out the last book I need...

"Hello," Tilly says.

Her tone is formal, as is her posture.

"Hello," I reply, matching her tone. "There you go again!"

"What did I do?" she asks.

"Just now, you gave me that pity look. I don't need a pity look from you or anyone else!"

"Wow, Jason said that you'd be resistant to truth. And I guess he was right."

I start laughing hysterically; it's a joyless laugh that comes from the deepest cave of Mount Sarcasm. I wave my arms in the air and address the whole school: "Did everyone hear that? Jason has an opinion about me! Well, you know what, Tilly, I have an opinion about Jason!"

"Fancy, don't you dare talk bad about him!"

I tug on my earlobe. "I'm sorry, I can't hear what you're saying because the buildings are talking so loudly."

"That's not funny."

"What's not funny is who you pretend to be when you're around him."

"I'm not pretending! I'm opening myself up to new situations. We're not all like you: stuck and afraid of any kind of change."

"You're pretending, and you know it. You don't care about any of the stuff that Jason likes. The only frequency you hear is whatever is playing on Spotify. Your dad wakes you up with the smell of bacon every Sunday! You literally have a bacon-shaped clock. I got you one for Christmas. And now you only eat veggie burgers? Why? Just because some guy says so?"

"Whatever, it's better than stalking some poor guy who doesn't know you exist!" she shoots back.

I ball my fists so tightly my nails cut into my palms. "I don't stalk! I admire from afar. Like bird watchers. I respect the subject I'm viewing and allow them their own space."

"Oh, please, you're one restraining order away from a misdemeanor!" she shouts.

"That's not true!" I reply.

"Why don't we ask Rahim?" she says. "Oh, wait, we can't. He's in hiding. From you."

I gasp as if she had reached out and punched me in the gut. I strike back. "Dean Koontz is a better horror writer than Edgar Allan Poe!"

She gasps, deeply shocked and hurt by my proclamation. "Statistically speaking, due to their difference in socioeconomic status and societal pressures, if Jack had lived, he and Rose would've been divorced within the year!"

"Take that back, Tilly!"

"No! And you know what else? Jason said that you had a very jealous aura. And I think he's right."

"I'm not jealous of you and Veggie Boy. I couldn't care less who you date! And tell Mr. Granola Nut Crunch to stay the heck out of my aura!" I march away and don't look back.

Now there's no way to avoid it. I *have* to make Imani like me in order to get that invite. It seemed like it was no big thing back in Mrs. Washington's office, but now, as I make my way down the hall, I can feel anxiety tighten my chest.

I walk to class in a haze. I would have walked right past it had it not been for my history teacher, Mr. Doyle, calling me out.

"And where are you going? Class has already started. Get inside," he says. I follow Mr. Doyle into class and take my seat.

"Good morning, everyone. I'll need your complete and total attention," Mr. Doyle says.

I have no idea what he says after that, because I zone out.

But unlike all the other times I've zoned out in class, this time I actually have a good reason: My world is collapsing right before my eyes. Everything that I used to know or believe in is suddenly a question mark.

How can so much change happen in the span of a few hours?

"Ms. Augustine!" Mr. Doyle yells, in a tone that tells me this is most likely not the first time that he has called my name.

"What?" I snap.

"Excuse me?" he demands. "Get your stuff and go to the principal's office right now!"

I see a flash of the principal in my head. He's calling my parents. I'm packing to go to Haiti.

I jump up out of my seat. "I'm so sorry, Mr. Doyle. I didn't mean to be disrespectful. I meant to ask 'what' in a very gentle, conformist way. I swear."

He grumbles, but then nods and says, "Fine, but you've been warned. And since you're already up, go ahead with your report on Haiti and why the Haitian Revolution was a key moment in history."

Damn it, the report! I forgot all about it! I need to ask Mr. Doyle for an extension, but one look at his face tells me that's not gonna happen.

"C'mon, get up here," he says.

"Well...see..."

"What is the issue, Fancy? I gave you this assignment specifically because I know it holds a personal connection for you."

"Fancy, you're Haitian?" the girl behind me asks.

I mumble, "Yes."

"So, do you know Voodoo and stuff? Can you do weird stuff like give a cat an extra leg?" Darren, a kid with thick glasses and ashy hands, asks.

"What? No! And why would I want to do that?" I reply.

"I don't know, for fun?" Darren says.

Note to self: Stay away from Darren and whatever may be in his freezer.

"What about curses? Can you put a curse on someone?" a voice says behind me.

"Fancy, can you do a love potion? Mark needs a date— badly," Nancy says, a few feet away. Mark wads up a sheet of paper and hurls it at her. The class laughs.

"For real, can you do a love potion?" Kenly, resident jock, asks, his eyes growing wide with wonder.

"Yo! How much? How much for a love potion?" Kenly's BFF Jack asks.

"Yeah, there're a few girls I been wanting to get to know better," Kenly says. The two of them exchange crude expressions and a fist bump.

"All right, all right, enough! Fancy, do you have the report or not?" Mr. Doyle asks.

I shake my head. "No."

He exhales and his shoulders slump. "This extra-credit assignment was to make up for all the other assignments that you missed. I'm disappointed in you, I really am. You're a bright girl, but if you don't apply yourself, none of that will matter."

Yeah, right. Like anything really matters anymore....

Mr. Doyle turns to the rest of the class. "I want all of you kids to find your personal connection with historical events. History matters."

I laugh sardonically. "Does it? Does it really matter? Because no matter how much history you have with a person, it won't stop them from throwing you away like a moldy hunk of cheese they found in the back of the fridge!"

Mr. Doyle looks at me, seriously confused. "What are you—"

"And you know what else about history? Everyone forgets it. They forget how you stayed up all night helping them find the perfect shade of black to paint their latest haunted mansion, even though it meant missing the season finale of *The Bachelor*!"

The more I talk, the tighter my chest gets. But I can't seem to stop myself. I feel hot tears make their way down my face, but there's no way I can stop them, either.

"And you know what else? They forget the time they had the flu and had to stay home without anyone to play with, so you kissed them on the cheek, just so you two could be sick together! Do they remember that history? NO!"

My voice is shaking and so are my hands. I want to control myself, but I can't. The words erupt out of me like I'm a volcano spewing lava down a mountain. The students—aka the villagers—look both amused and a little scared. They should run.

The room is frozen in complete disbelief. It takes the class a few seconds to decide how they'll react to my outburst. In the end, they decide on the response that has served countless high school students well for generations—laughter. The entire class is howling with laughter.

The bell rings. Mr. Doyle dismisses everyone but me.

I keep my head down, but I hear them shuffling out of class, still laughing and making fun of the odd, nutty girl who lost it in history class. The last thing I hear a student say as they walk out is, "I bet she is a Voodoo witch. If I were Mr. Doyle, I wouldn't want to be alone with her."

It's just Mr. Doyle and me now. I hear him coming closer to me. He sits on top of the desk in front of mine.

"Falencia, it's okay. Everything is okay."

"No, it's not," I mumble into the desk. I'm not even sure he understood what I said.

"Yes, it is. You can look at me. I understand what's going on."

I slowly raise my head and make eye contact with Mr. Doyle. Can it be? Does he *really* understand? Maybe he's a deep, empathetic teacher with an almost superhuman ability to understand and sympathize with distraught teenagers like me.

Maybe Mr. Doyle is really my own personal Morpheus, Dumbledore, or even...Yoda! The next words out of his mouth will be so earth-shattering and wise, they'll set my whole life onto a new path—a path to a glorious, Oprah-like revelation!

"Fancy..."

"Yes, Mr. Doyle?" I reply, eagerly awaiting his sage words.

"How much *do* you charge for a love potion?"

Without saying a word, I march out of class. There are only two topics being discussed in the halls of Ellen Craft High—Imani's party and the Voodoo witch who had a meltdown. It turns out both topics make me want to quit high school. What's worse is that a few of the kids call out my name and ask for me to do something "witchlike." I don't even bother to roll my eyes. I just keep stomping down the hall, mission-oriented. I know exactly where I'm going and what I need to do there.

I head for the cafeteria, where six staff are tidying up after breakfast. They look up as soon as I enter. I don't bother with them; I go straight to the boss—the head lunch lady, Ms. Hattie.

Ms. Hattie is five foot three and looks like she could blow away with the smallest gust of wind. But don't let that fool you—she plays no games.

She's wiping down the tables, and before I can even ask, she says, "No."

"Please?" I beg.

She looks up at me. Her expression softens, and she gestures toward the kitchen. I enter and grab the full-length puffy coat hanging on the wall.

There's staff milling around, getting ready for lunch. I walk past them and into the oversized, soundproof chrome freezer.

"ARRRRRRRRRRRRGH!"

I scream, over and over again. It's not enough; it will never be enough.

I jam my fist into a tall sack of flour leaning on the wall of the freezer. I pound on it over and over again. I should have seen it coming—there's no way an innocent sack of flour could bear the brunt of my rage. The sack burps up a torrent of flour clouds; they cover me from head to toe.

I open the freezer door, and the whole staff turns to face me. I'm guessing I look like a Black Cruella de Vil caught in a snowstorm. I hold my flour-coated head high and march out of the kitchen.

I walk by Ms. Hattie and stop. She doesn't look shocked or the least bit taken aback by my appearance. We exchange a stoic look and nod toward each other.

"Ms. Hattie."

"Fancy."

CHAPTER 9

On my way to the bathroom to clean up, I'm stopped two separate times by students. They ask why I'm covered in flour, and does it have to do with Voodoo. I ignore both of them and keep walking. Once in the bathroom, I quickly wipe away the flour. The door opens, and out of all the girls at Ellen Craft High, it's none other than Imani.

She eyes me with disdain as she washes her hands. Well, I might as well get this over with. I go over what to say in my head.

"Hey, Imani. I love the way your fangs glisten in the sunlight. Does that happen to all soul-sucking serpents, or just you?"

Okay, that's not it.

"Imani, I love your boots! Did Satan pick them out for you himself? Or did all his underlings get new footwear?"

Try again…

I take a deep breath and roll my shoulders back a few times, to relax.

I manage to choke out, "Imani, I love your hair!"

"Yeah, I know. It's glorious, as always," she says.

"Girl, you're so funny." Wow, I'm bad at this.

She studies me. "What's wrong with you? Why are you trying to suck up to me?"

My jaw drops. "Me? That's not what I'm doing."

She arches her expertly sculpted eyebrows and folds her arms across her chest.

"Well, maybe a little. But that's only because you're so stunning," I reply. I feel so dirty. I'm gonna need holy water and a priest who enjoys a challenge to feel clean again.

"Enough. Just tell me what you want," she demands.

It's now or never. . . .

"I was hoping you'd give me an invite to your—"

Before I can finish, she breaks out in a fit of laughter, the kind that produces actual tears. The smart thing to do is to laugh it off, too, and keep trying to get on her good side.

That does not happen.

"This was just a waste of time. I don't know why I thought you'd even say yes. You hate me, and you've made that very clear—for years now. I didn't hit you with that soccer ball on purpose. But every day I feel less and less guilty about it."

"You made me look like a country hick in my own school picture! That's permanent," she retorts.

"It was an accident. But you wouldn't understand that because you don't have accidents and you don't make mistakes. You are the great Imani Parker, the queen of all things perfect. But the rest of us out here, we make mistakes. We have faults."

We lie to our best friends....

"I'm sorry, I'm not sure why that should be any of my concern," she says, genuinely indifferent.

A thought occurs to me, one that hadn't crossed my mind before. I look at Imani real hard and don't break eye contact.

"I just now understood who you really are—you're a dictator in an authoritarian system. The kind of dictator who is afraid to let her people gather in protest or read history books for fear they will rise up and overthrow you," I inform her.

She looks confused.

I grunt and start to explain. "Authoritarianism is—"

"I know what authoritarianism is! I get better grades than you in history. In fact, I get better grades than you in everything. I'm a straight A student."

"I don't care— Wait, really?"

"Yes," she says in a matter-of-fact tone.

"Okay, that's impressive. But my point still stands—you're like a cruel dictator. You fear giving the people access. Because if we were given access and opportunity, we'd start a coup and overthrow you!"

"You really think that?" she asks.

"Well, yeah. I do!"

She looks me up and down from head to toe. "It's not easy to be this beautiful all the time. And it's not just about looks. I have to maintain stability and preserve our way of life at Ellen Craft High. If you don't know who is the most beloved, most envied, and most sought-after girl in the school, how will you know who to compare yourself to? It's easy to paint me as a mean girl, but that's not the case. Fancy, I'm not the enemy; I'm the goal."

Did she really just say that?

"ARGH! Waste of time," I spit angrily. I go for the door and turn the knob.

"Wait!" she shouts.

I don't bother to turn and face her. "What?"

"Access and opportunity, huh? Okay, I'll give you what you want. You can come to my party."

I whip around and face her. It's possible that I'm currently in some kind of hallucinogenic state and this is only my mind playing tricks on me. So, to confirm, I ask her again.

"Did you just say I can come to your party?"

"Yes." She goes over to her handbag and takes out a red envelope.

OMG! It's happening? It's happening!

She hands me the envelope. "Here. Now you have access and opportunity. Let's see how well your rebellion goes."

My hands are trembling as I reach out for it. I half expect her to take it back and laugh, saying it was all a joke.

I thank her, and she simply gives me a small nod. Well, I'm

no fool. I need to get out of here as fast as I can. It's like robbing a bank. When you're done, you don't hang out in the parking lot to see if any of the tellers want to get Thai with you.

My heart is beating ten times faster than it should and my fingers are still shaky. I quickly open the door and step out into the hallway.

Imani follows me. "Fancy, just one thing. You have to bring a guy to the party. And not just a friend or some loser relative. You need to be in a real relationship."

"Wait, are you saying..."

"That's right. This year it's couples only. Anyone who wants to get into my party will have to come with a boyfriend or girlfriend."

"And what if—for argument's sake—you don't have a boyfriend?" I ask, keeping my tone light and breezy.

She smiles. "Well, I guess you better get one—quick."

I have an invite! I'm supposed to feel utter elation right now, but I don't. How am I going to do in a few weeks what I haven't been able to do in years? Get a boyfriend, really? Why does everything always come with an asterisk? Why must there be some awful fine print? *C'mon, White Jesus, why couldn't You just give me this one?*

The closer I get to my locker, the more miserable I feel. It doesn't help that a kid sees me in the hall and shouts,

"Voodoo girl! What's up?" The girl he's with thinks it's funny to add, "I need to put a spell on Mr. Norm. Do witches take Cash App?"

I grit my teeth. Idiot.

I see my locker just ahead; the only saving grace is that Tilly isn't there. While it would be great to wave the invite in her face, she would surely spot the sadness behind my petty jester façade. I'm eager to get my stuff and go. I can't take running into Tilly right now.

I'm rushing to shove everything in my backpack when someone taps my shoulder from behind. I have no doubt it's yet another student who wants to tease me about Voodoo, so I turn around and bark, "Leave me alone!"

The person on the other end of my outburst is Rahim. Suddenly, everything around us—the lockers, the classrooms, the hallway—blurs. He is the only thing in focus.

Run!

I am about to do just that when I ask myself, *When will I have another chance to have a conversation with Rahim?*

There are a number of things I can say to him right now. But I make sure to think before I open my mouth. I caution myself against saying anything goofy or even slightly embarrassing.

"I'm not stalking you," I blurt out.

"What?" he replies, clearly confused.

"I just wanted you to know that. I'm not a stalker. I'm normal. Very, very normal," I add, almost starting to believe it myself.

"Okay..."

I clear my throat and try again. "What's up?" I ask, hoping I sound casual and unbothered.

"You're Fancy, right?"

"Yeah...?" I reply, uneasy.

"Some of my boys are in your history class. They said you're some kind of Voodoo witch and you make potions."

"ARGH! I'm not! Why can't anyone in this school just let that dumb rumor go? It's a lie!"

He puts his hands up and says, "My bad. Guess I heard wrong." He starts to walk away.

"Rahim, wait..."

He turns back and gives me his full attention.

"I *am* a Voodoo witch," I say.

WTH, Fancy?

"You just said the rumor wasn't true," he points out.

I shrug. "I don't want everyone begging me to make them a potion. You know how it goes. This one wants perfect grades; that one wants a million Insta followers. It gets to be too much."

He takes a beat before he answers. I think he's trying to figure out if I'm lying to him or not. He's so close I can smell his scent—raindrops, candlelight, and love.

He whispers, "Does that stuff really work?"

"Yeah. Totally."

Does Hell get Netflix? I'm pretty sure that's where I'm going.

"Could you make a potion for me?" he asks.

"What do you want it to do?"

He comes in even closer. I have to hold myself back from leaning in and kissing him. I control myself enough that I don't act on my urges, but my heart rate is through the roof and I'm sweating all over.

"I need a potion that makes someone fall out of love. You have something like that?" he asks, sounding apprehensive.

"Ah, yeah. I think so. Who are you trying to stop being in love with?"

He shifts his weight, and for the first time since I've been following him, Rahim seems unsure of himself. "It's not for me. It's for someone else, and I can't tell you who. How much would it cost?"

The bell rings and everyone begins to rush off to their next class. Okay, it's time to come clean. But before I can confess, I see Imani over Rahim's shoulders. She gives me her trademark snarky smile and taps on her swanky watch, letting me know the clock is ticking. It's in that moment that I know I'm about to do something brave. And by brave, I mean totally ill-advised and stupid.

I turn my focus back to Rahim. "Actually, I don't want money. I'll make you a potion if you pretend to be my boyfriend. That way I can go to Imani's party."

"You want a pretend boyfriend?" he asks, probably assuming he heard wrong.

"Yeah." I look back at Imani. She's no longer looking at me. She's too busy having some guy swoon over her. "I don't want a one-time thing on the night of the party. I want everything on the boyfriend/girlfriend menu—well, not *everything*..."

"Yeah, I get it. You want everyone to think I'm your dude."

I'm so lost in his eyes that all I can manage is a nod.

"I saw this movie once and the woman made a magic potion to get revenge on a guy who betrayed her. And to complete the potion, she added an item that belonged to him. Are you going to need something like that?"

I have no idea....

"Ah yeah, of course. I'll definitely need a personal item from the person who is supposed to fall out of love. And then I'll take care of the rest," I reply.

Dear White Jesus, tell me he bought that.

"Okay. What happens once the potion is made? How do I get it to work? Do I put it in water and get them to drink it or...what?"

Suddenly, my mind flashes back to a random episode of *Dateline* I watched with my mom, where the wife put drops of poison in her husband's shampoo.

"Every witch has a different method when it comes to stuff like that. The kinds of potions I make are...topical. So, all you would have to do is add a drop into the person's hand lotion or shower gel...and it starts working," I add.

"Right away or slowly over time?"

"It works fast," I reply.

"Great! I'll get you the personal item. How soon after that can I get the potion?"

"After Imani's party. Deal?" I ask.

He quietly thinks it over and then says, "Yeah, we have a deal."

There are four words ringing in my head that both thrill and terrify me: What. Will. I. Wear. It has to be something that is worthy of this momentous occasion. An outfit that is so regal, so otherworldly, it'll rip the very breath from everyone's lungs and leave them gasping for air. A gown so glorious, both Time and Imani will be forced to stop and admire me as I make my grand entrance. In short, I'm looking for the dress that'll topple the Imani Empire once and for all.

And I need that dress to be under two hundred dollars. That's the amount I have saved up from my allowance and previous birthday money. I set it aside as a Romance Lovers Book-Con fund, but this party is more important. I begin scouring the internet and spend two whole hours looking. So far, I've found some pretty dresses but nothing with the impact that I'm looking for.

As much as I would like to keep searching, I have other things that must be done besides shopping.

My first instinct is to find a way to fake the potion, but I decide against it. I've already lied once; I don't want to add yet another lie to our relationship. That kind of couple never gets a happy ending. I'm going to learn how to make a potion and give our budding relationship a fighting chance.

I Google the best Voodoo shop in Brooklyn, and it leads me to Papa Juju.

Voodoo is a religion that came from Africa and was brought to Haiti by enslaved people in the sixteenth century. It's a faith centered on nature, balance, and spirituality. That's the Wiki version. But to hear my mom tell it, Voodoo is a direct line to evil. If you mess with it, unspeakable things will happen. The theory is that you might get what you want, but at a steep price.

When my mom was little, she'd overhear the village elders tell stories of Voodoo. They involved ravenous mystical creatures, zombies, and demon possessions. The people in the stories didn't survive if they didn't have some form of protection.

I'm not saying the stories are true. But just in case, I take out my cell and zoom in on a picture where White Jesus can clearly be seen in the background. I make that picture my home screen—can't be too careful.

My heart pounds loudly in my ears, the closer I get to the store. I tell myself it's just a regular shop and I need to relax. I carefully open the door. The shop is adorned with African masks, Voodoo dolls, and skulls. In the corner, there's a life-size statue of a man with the head of a goat. The grimace on the goatman's face sends goose bumps down my arms. I scold myself for being on edge. How scary can the place be if they take Apple Pay?

Ceremonial trays with carvings of pentagrams surround me. I spot an entire shelf dedicated to miniature coffins. I can't help but think about Tilly. This place would be like Christmas for her. I choke down my sadness and focus on the mission.

I approach the man behind the counter, who wears a colorful patterned shirt and an avalanche of beaded chains.

"How can I help you?" he says. His Haitian Creole accent is subtle, but I pick it up right away.

"I need a book on how to make potions," I whisper, as if my mom were in the shop with me and might overhear.

He gives me a small smile. "So, you want to study what our ancestors called Vodun? I have several books that will help you begin what will be approximately a two-year journey."

I twist my face in disbelief. "Two years? I was hoping you had something that could help me by tonight."

"I'm sorry, that is not possible. There is so much to cover— we're talking centuries of tradition and customs."

"Do you have, like, a 'quick guide to being a witch' kind of thing? Maybe something I can download?"

The man snarls, "Are you asking if there's a Voodoo app?"

"Yes! That would be perfect."

"No. We don't have an app," he says in a tone that lets me know I'm trying his patience.

I sigh. "Okay. Then point me to the potions. I'm looking for something that makes someone fall out of love."

"That is a complex mixture that involves blending many different herbs, oils, and not to mention sacrifice."

My mouth goes dry and goose bumps form down my arms. "Someone has to be killed to make the potion?"

He laughs. "No, this is not the movies. There are many other forms of sacrifice."

"Okay, good to know. Lead the way," I tell him.

He takes me to the back room, where several glass bottles are on display. He hands me one about the size of my palm. Inside is a red liquid with herbs.

"So this will make a person stop loving someone?" I ask.

"Exactly."

I really tried the honest route, but I just don't have years to dedicate to this. Rahim doesn't need to know that I didn't make the potion. All that matters is I have something to give him.

"I'll take one bottle. How much?"

"Two hundred and forty-two dollars—before tax."

"SERIOUSLY?"

"Good morning!"

The sound of my voice startles Mrs. Washington as she walks out of the Starbucks a few blocks from the school. She nearly drops the coffee she's holding.

"Sorry."

"Fancy, what are you doing here?"

"I had to drop off some stuff for my mom at the dry cleaner's. I saw you in the window, and I thought—"

"You thought you'd scare the daylights out of me?" she says, wiping the rim of her coffee cup.

"Again, sorry."

"It's fine. Whatever you need to talk to me about, can it wait until school actually starts in twenty minutes?" she asks.

"I was going to do that. But then I thought it might be a good idea to approach you now and get you while you're still fresh!"

"Fresh?" Mrs. Washington mutters, "I really need to set some boundaries."

I pout and offer her an out. "If you want, I can see you later in your office. You probably have a full day and won't be able to fit me in for a few hours...and, well, who knows what will have become of me a few hours from now?"

She rolls her eyes. "Nothing will become of you. You'll have a normal day, just like any other day."

"I bet that's what the people of Pompeii thought on the day Mount Vesuvius erupted. There they were, living their lives, and then boom—they all turned to ash."

"Fine. You have the next three blocks until we get to school. Then you will go straight to class. And I do not want to see you for the rest of the day. Got it?"

"Thank you!" We start to walk, and I tell her all about my deal with Rahim.

"What? Fancy, you can't lie to him like that."

"It won't be a lie for long," I assure her.

"What does that mean?" she asks. I tell her about my visit to the Voodoo shop.

"So the shop owner told you how expensive the potion was. Then you came to your senses and told Rahim the truth?"

"C'mon, we both know that is not my brand."

She sighs. "Yes, but I keep hoping."

"I told Rahim that I would make him a potion, and I am not a quitter, Mrs. Washington. In this case, I aim—in the immortal words of Tennyson—to strive, to seek, to find, and not to yield!"

"That's a literary way of saying you plan to continue lying?"

I nod reluctantly. "Yeah, pretty much..."

I recount what happened after I recovered from the shock of the price of the potion. The storeowner held up a book on the basics of Voodoo potion making, written by a Haitian professor. It was an acclaimed book with detailed information not only on making potions but also on the true history of Voodoo.

"So you bought the book?" she asks.

"I didn't. Because it had been out of print for a while, it was almost forty bucks! Luckily, I found this at the used bookstore not far from the Voodoo shop." I take a book out of my backpack and show her.

She reads the title out loud. "*One Hundred and One Voodoo Spells from Popular TV & Film.* So instead of getting a book written by someone who actually knows the history and culture, you picked a book that looks like it was stapled together at Office Depot by some guy who, according to this blurb, 'plans to go to Haiti someday'?"

"Well, yeah. It was only four ninety-nine!"

She exhales and signals for me to continue.

"So I went home to make my very own potion. The mixture I was looking for was toward the back of the book. It called for black chicken feathers, red candles, white crystals, ten different essential oils, and the blood of a goat. The book had an easy-to-follow diagram of how to set up the altar. At the center of the altar should be a sacred bowl that the potion maker holds dear."

"You had all those things lying around the house?" Mrs. Washington asks.

"Not everything. I had some of the oils, but the other stuff I had to improvise. For the chicken feather, I used a feather from a pair of old earrings I had back when I was still searching for my personal style. I don't think it's a chicken feather, but close enough. I used my mom's candles from Bath & Body Works. And for the goat blood, my mom is making goat stew tonight, so she left the meat out to defrost and I scraped some frozen blood off it. As for the sacred bowl, well, I don't think anything could be more sacred to me than my Stewie Griffin cereal bowl."

"Oh, Fancy..."

"I know, clever, right?"

"Just...keep going," she says.

"I thought I would test it out first on my dad to see if it worked. I got the laces from his old tennis shoe and put them inside the bowl. Then I did what the book said and concentrated really hard on something I wanted him to stop loving—sugar.

My mom is always complaining he puts too much of it in his coffee. So I held the picture of sugar in my mind. I was ready.

"Just picture it, Mrs. Washington: There I am, in my room, and it's almost midnight. The book didn't say it had to be night, but it felt right. I put everything in place and then began to chant, '*Give me power over the mind! Give me power over the mind!*' in Haitian Creole. I lit the match and dropped it into the bowl. And then, according to the book, I needed to close my eyes. And so I did."

Mrs. Washington stops walking and turns to face me. "What happened?"

"I heard the sound of thunder, out of nowhere!"

"Really?" she says incredulously.

"Yes! It had to be a sign the potion was working—or so I thought. In actuality, my mom had just turned on her sound machine. It helps her sleep."

Mrs. Washington bursts out laughing.

"It could have been Voodoo thunder. It just so happened that it wasn't," I argue.

She tries to compose herself. "I'm sorry, Fancy. So what happened after you chanted and chanted?"

"Remember I had to light the match and close my eyes? Well, that might not have been a great idea," I reply as I pull out a few strands of my hair from under my hat and show them to her.

Mrs. Washington gasps. "Fancy! You singed your hair off!"

"Just a little. It was time I got a new hairstyle anyway."

She is about to say something but bites her tongue at the last second.

"The book said if I did everything right, the potion should turn blood red. The closest it got was a dark reddish brown. But I figured that was good enough.

"I followed the directions exactly: I held the picture of sugar in my mind and then put one drop of the potion into my dad's slipper. I woke up this morning and my dad poured his coffee and didn't add sugar!"

She stops walking. "So you think it worked?"

"No, turns out we were just out of sugar. But I'm not giving up. I buried all the Voodoo stuff under my bed. So I can try again."

Mrs. Washington gets this faraway look on her face.

"Mrs. Washington, you okay?"

"Yeah, I was just wondering why I didn't go into nursing. . . ."

CHAPTER 10

I find a dress close to what I had in mind, but it's the wrong color. I want something shimmering—silver or gold. I want it to make a statement. I keep looking for another hour. My cell dings, reminding me about my date with Rahim. Yeah, right. Like I needed to be reminded that I get to meet up with the boy of my dreams. It was all I could do to concentrate earlier at school today. I go to the back of my closet and take out a stash I was able to sneak past my mom last year: cute short skirt, dark ruby-red lipstick, and a low-cut top. I'm so relieved both of my parents are working late. If not, I would have had to bring a change of clothes with me.

I look myself over in the mirror. "Okay, White Jesus, how do I look?"

WJ scoffs at me.

"On second thought, keep your opinions to yourself!"

White Jesus has questions.

I groan and reply, "Yes, I'm going to meet him at the same pizza shop Tilly and I used to go to all the time. And yes, I'm hoping she's there so I can rub it in her face, but c'mon, I'm human. Aren't I allowed to order a small side dish of pettiness? Once in a while?"

He gives me the side-eye.

"Fine, judge me from the comfort of Your cozy poster. You have no idea what it's like out here!"

When I enter the pizza shop, the first person I look for isn't Rahim, it's Tilly. I need her to see me here with Rahim. That way, she'll never give me that pity look again. Unfortunately, she's nowhere around. Damn it!

I scold myself for even thinking about Tilly at this very moment. She's just a footnote in my sweeping romance saga. I'm here for Rahim.

The bell hanging over the door of the shop rings. I know it's Rahim even before I lay eyes on him. There are goose bumps running down my arms. And I can't believe how fast my heart is beating.

He's wearing dark jeans and a rust-colored jacket that

brings out the amber flecks in his eyes. His hair is stacked up in a spiky ponytail, and his locs are, as always, freshly twisted. He complements his look with a pair of tan and white Jordans. He walks over; swagger is off the charts.

Then he tilts his chin up toward me. "What's up?"

I remind myself that I have been preparing for this moment and that I am more than capable of being cool.

"I love you!" The words tumble out of my mouth before I can stop them.

"What?" he asks.

OMG! Someone kill me! Now!

"I'd love you—to take a seat. Here, at the table. Where I am also sitting," I reply, hoping to cover up my huge mistake.

"Are you gonna order anything?" he asks.

"I'll get a slice later."

He turns and walks up to the counter to place his order. I refuse to let this meeting be a disaster. I must take control. And it doesn't matter how nervous I am or how fast my heart is racing—I will not let this evening end badly.

Rahim comes back with two slices of sausage-and-mushroom pizza and a drink. He takes a seat. He pulls something out of his back pocket and slides it over to me—a blue striped tie. "What's this for?" I ask.

"You said you needed a personal item, remember?"

"Oh! Yeah! Right. I was kidding. Of course I know what it's for. The potion." I laugh awkwardly. I take it from him. I'd like to ask who it belongs to, but he doesn't give me a chance.

"Now that you have the tie, you can get started, right?" he asks.

"Yes, I'm all set."

"Good. Hey, don't you have other guys you follow around besides me? Could they have pretended to be your boyfriend?"

"I don't follow you or anyone around," I object.

He looks at me and furrows his brow.

"I don't! If you happened to see me behind you or something—we just happened to be going in the same direction. It's a small school," I point out. I want so desperately to hide under the table.

He shrugs. "Okay. You weren't following me."

"Why would I do that? You think I'm that kind of girl? You know what, forget it. This was a bad idea," I reply as I stand up and hand him the tie.

My knees are weak and my hands are shaking from a mixture of anger and sheer embarrassment. How could I be so stupid as to think this would work? I start walking out of the shop.

He quickly gets up and follows me. "Wait! My bad. I wasn't trying to come for you like that. I was wondering why you didn't just ask another guy." He hands me back the tie. I take it from him. He seems sincere enough. Still, I need to make sure.

"If we do this, we need to lay down some ground rules," I say. "Rule one: You can't back out."

"Okay, fine. I won't."

"Good. And the second rule is: No one must know about our agreement."

"Done," he says. "I have a third rule."

I wasn't expecting him to say that. "What is it?"

"Do not ask or try to find out who I want to give the potion to. That's my business. Got it?"

"I won't ask," I promise. Damn. Now I really want to know who he's going to give the potion to. But I need this thing to go well, so I push my curiosity aside and stay focused. "We need to talk about how we're gonna sell the idea that we're dating— how did we meet?" I ask.

He shrugs. "At school."

I scrunch my face and turn my nose up at his suggestion. "I refuse to have a boring meet-cute," I inform him.

"A meet-cute? C'mon, that's for people who fall in love and all that. That's not us. Just say something about how you and I bumped into each other and then started hanging out. Done."

I roll my eyes. "What's next? You tell them how we had our first kiss near the dumpster out back?"

He pulls back and says, "Nah, I was gonna tell them we made out by the pile of laundry near the boys' locker room. And for our first date, I took you to the subway to see which one of us could spot the most rats."

"ARGH! Is that the best you can do? You're not even try-ing!" I snap.

"I was joking."

"We are talking about romance. There's no room for jokes."

"Okay, tell me your version."

I take a deep breath, close my eyes, and work my magic.

"It was a cold and rainy night. I was at the bus stop. The bus arrived and I was about to be splashed with dirty rainwater. You came out of nowhere and put your jacket in the puddle so I could walk over it. Then we looked into each other's eyes and fell instantly in love."

Rahim bursts out laughing. He's laughing so hard he can barely hold himself together.

"There's nothing funny about the way we met," I reply.

"That depends—did we meet this century?" he says.

I force myself to take a breath and stay calm. "All right, fine. What would you like to change about our story?"

"Everything!" he replies. "Why would I ruin a perfectly good jacket?"

"So that I don't get splashed by the muddy water!"

"You've been at the bus stop on a rainy night, with no umbrella. You're already wet. What's a few more drops? And there's no way I'm about to get my kicks wet."

"Sneakers? You're worried about your sneakers when the love of your life is in danger?"

He points toward his feet. "Not just sneakers, Jordans. And since when was a puddle considered dangerous? Just jump over it."

"So what would you rather our story be? You came up to me and said, '*Yo, I'm sayin', Ma, let's do this.*' And then we ended up making out in some dark, filthy alley near the dollar store?"

"You don't ever go to the dollar store?"

"Yeah, for cheap Popsicles. I don't go there to fall in love."

"Whatever. Tell the school whatever you want about us. Just make sure that potion works," he says, throwing the rest of his food into the trash bin nearby.

"Fine, I'll tell them whatever I want. And you just agree with it."

"Fine!" he says, heading toward the exit.

"I'm glad it's not real because I'd never say yes to you in real life. Not with that attitude."

"Don't worry, I'd *never* ask you out! I don't date delusional romantics." He opens the door and storms out.

I run to the door and call out after him, "And I don't date sanctimonious sneakerheads!"

ARGH! I hate him!

I jump onto my bed, put my face in the pillow, and scream. When I'm done, I turn over and stare at the ceiling. How could I have been so blind about Rahim? I let his toned body, impeccable smile, and infinite charm fool me into thinking he was a good guy.

Rahim isn't a good guy at all. In fact, he's a first-class jerk!

Maybe this is a good thing. Now that I know he's an awful guy, I really will be pretending. And I won't be in any danger of falling for him and getting my heart broken. In fact, I vow to stay away from Rahim unless we are in school and are forced to have to pretend for Imani.

"Fancy! Come down here now!" Mom yells.

"Coming!"

"Falencia Marie Augustine, I said now!"

I bolt upright and run down the stairs like my life depends on it. My mom rarely uses my full name, and when she does, it's never followed by something good.

When I get downstairs, I head to the kitchen, where I can hear her and my dad talking. I enter and see my parents are looking at something on my mom's cell phone.

"What's going on?" I ask.

"You tell us." Mom shows me the picture that she and my dad are looking at. It's a photo of me in a miniskirt, with red lips and revealing top, just before I walked into the pizza shop. My mind spins, trying to think of how they could have gotten this.

It doesn't matter how; the point is they have it. How do you get out of it?

"Where did you get these clothes?" Dad says.

I shrug and look down at the floor.

"Do not make us ask you again," Mom warns. She starts switching between English and Haitian Creole. How lucky am I to get scolded in two different languages?

"Your mother is talking to you! Answer her," Dad barks.

"I bought them online," I admit. "I think *maybe* I forgot to ask your permission, but I—"

"Stop talking!" Mom explodes.

I wisely stay quiet.

"You're not allowed to dress like that. You broke our rules. And that is unacceptable," Dad says.

"I'm sitting here, getting dinner ready, and I get a message from Sister Marie-Jean, this picture that she took while she was out. She asked when I started to let you dress like you had no upbringing."

"Tell us this, Fancy. Who are you dressing like that for?" Dad asks.

"No one. Why is it so hard to get you two to listen to me? All I'm doing is trying to be like everyone else. What is wrong with having a life?"

"You have a life—I know because I gave it to you," Mom says. "I remember the fourteen hours of labor. Trust me, I was there. But that very life I gave you, I can take it away."

I actually feel my blood boiling. I desperately want to break something. I would do just about anything to run off, but I know it would make things worse. So I stand there and hope this torment will be over soon.

"I'll only ask you this once. Do not lie to us. Do you have a boyfriend?" Dad asks.

"No."

"You better not," Mom says. "We didn't bring you to this country to hang out and have boyfriends. Education. That's the goal. And I will make sure you stay on that path if I have to walk behind you every step. Do you understand, Falencia?"

"Yes, Mom."

"Go upstairs and bring down the clothes you've been hiding."

I turn toward the door, but before I can leave, she adds, "And hurry up! You're coming to church with me tonight."

"What? But I have school tomorrow!"

"You'll be home in plenty of time to get some sleep. Let's go!"

When you Google "Haitian churches in Brooklyn," almost twenty places show up. But in reality, there are about eight hundred of them. That's because most of our churches are makeshift. They could be in the basement of someone's home, the back of someone's yard, or a storefront. Our church is on the ground floor of a small two-story community center. They added folding chairs, a podium, and a microphone: instant church.

I don't mind coming here. We have a dope choir, I like reading out loud from the Bible sometimes, and I even pray. The only thing I do mind is the length of the service. I think I'd do really well in, like, a "drive-through church." I can see it now: Our car pulls up to the window. We say what sins we're sorry for. And then we turn the corner and forgiveness is waiting in the next window. But no one else shares my desire for express absolution.

Mom and I walk toward the blue banner marked GREAT SHEPHERD & HOPE CHURCH. We enter and encounter the same three ladies we always see when we first arrive—the Jacob sisters. They remind me of the three witches in *Macbeth*. I would not go so far as to say they are evil. However, the way they huddle up and whisper as people enter, the way they cackle when the other tells a joke...I wouldn't put anything past them.

They're the oldest members of the congregation and sit perched in their favorite spot—behind the welcome table, right by the entrance. On the table are extra Bibles, pamphlets of upcoming church events, and a sign-up sheet for confession, testimonials, and solo performances. The Jacob sisters have just two hobbies: gossiping and competing to see which one of them is the closest to death.

My mom greets them with a simple "Good evening," but because I'm "just a kid," I have to take more formal steps: I reach over the table and kiss each sister on the cheek. It's a sign of respect. Once when I was nine, I had to pee so badly when I got here, I ran straight for the restroom. For the next four Sundays, all they did was whisper to each other, loud enough for me to hear, "Well, Fancy is too grown to greet us properly. She's just so...American now." Mom made me go over to their house and bring them an apology pineapple upside-down cake.

"The other ladies are getting the refreshments ready for after service. Can you go and help them in the back?" the oldest sister asks my mom. She agrees. I start to follow her quickly, because the last thing I want is to be stuck with the three sisters. They like to ask us "young people" how we are, but it's really just a pretense so they can tell you what's wrong with them. Mom and I sometimes joke about it, as do most of the people in our church. She even admitted to me once that she dreaded running into them in the supermarket because they do the same thing to her.

I'm almost out of the danger zone when my mom turns back and says, "Fancy, I can help with the food, you go and keep the sisters company."

My jaw drops; her betrayal cuts deep. Mom smirks and walks away. This punishment is way too severe for the "crime" of wearing a short skirt and makeup. I thought my mom loved me. The sisters cheer.

"Oh good! Come, Fancy!" the youngest says.

"Hurry, before the service starts," the middle one adds.

"How are you feeling?" the oldest sister inquires.

And so it begins: They ask how I am. I give them a courteous and succinct answer. Then they wait for me to ask how they are. A diatribe of illnesses ranging from the common cold to the black plague soon follows.

Don't get me wrong—if they were sick, I would feel bad. But they have a habit of self-diagnosing and then leaping to the only conclusion that seems logical to them—death. Well, I will not play that game today.

"Fancy, my sister asked how you are," the youngest says.

"Um...I'm good, thank you," I reply.

The silence grows.

I don't care. I can take it if they can. Every second that

passes, it's harder for me to stay in the fight. Finally, unable to take the quiet, I yield.

"And how are you feeling, Aunties?" I ask.

The next twenty minutes are a blur of complaints about pain they experience in various places in their bodies.

I relent. "Oh, I'm so sorry to hear that. You Aunties are very brave. I feel awful that you're all so ill. I'll pray for you."

I thought that was the end. I was wrong. The oldest sister wants me to know all about her gallbladder operation from last year. That's when I think death won't be so bad; anything other than this. Thankfully the music begins, letting us know it's time for service. We enter the room. The sisters take a seat behind Mom. The oldest one whispers to her, "We had a lovely talk with Fancy. I was going to tell her about my operation, but another time."

Mom looks at me pointedly and says to the sisters, "Well, Fancy has time after church. She can walk you ladies home, that way you can tell her the rest of the story. And any other story you'd like to share. She loves talking to all of you."

I lean over and whisper in Mom's ear. "Well played, Mrs. Augustine. Well played."

I text Rahim first thing the next morning and tell him that we're supposed to walk into school holding hands so everyone can see. I also insist we add each other to all our social media because that's the first thing a real couple would do.

He texts me back, *k*. I reply, *You're so eloquent in the morning.* He texts me back an eye-rolling emoji.

Whatever.

It's half past seven, we're standing in front of the school entrance. It looks like most of the student body is here. Rahim and I exchange a nod and then hold hands. Yes, his hand feels warm and cozy, and yes, this was once a fantasy of mine. But now that I know who he really is, Rahim is no more than a means to an end. Although I can't lie—he really does smell good. And there's the matter of his piercing eyes....

Focus, Fancy!

We walk down the hall, gazing lovingly into each other's eyes, right past Imani and her nagging, gossipy crows. She actually drops her books, and her face proceeds to slide down to the floor. It takes both Cheer and Echo to help her pick her face back up. It is, in a word, beautiful.

And she isn't the only one—I literally see a student doing a spit take! There's a crescendo of gasps and whispers.

"Falencia, my office!" Mrs. Washington's voice rings out behind me.

I'm guessing I'm being called into her office because she saw Rahim and me walking down the hall, his arm now wrapped around my waist.

I say goodbye to Rahim and enter Mrs. Washington's office.

I take a seat. She sits on the edge of her desk with her arms firmly folded across her chest, wearing a serious expression.

"So...what's up?" I ask casually, as if I have no idea what this meeting could be about.

Mrs. Washington gives me a look that tells me she fails to appreciate the way my mind works. She comes and sits right next to me instead of directly across, like she usually does. "You really are going through with this? What if he falls for you only to learn you have been lying to him?"

I told her about our meetup yesterday and how much we argued. I promise her this is just a business arrangement. There's no way we would fall for each other.

"This plan of yours isn't a good idea."

"Why not?"

"Are you really asking me why this scheme is a bad idea?"

"Okay, I get how it could maybe backfire, but it won't! I got this."

"Fancy, this isn't just about you. I see a lot of kids in my office, and they have very real issues. You don't know what other students are going through and what challenges they may be facing. I want you to remember that Rahim isn't just some cute guy you daydream about. He's a person. And you need to be careful how you treat him."

"Yeah, sure. Okay." I shrug, not really sure what she's getting at.

"Dare I ask about the homework assignments?" she says.

"Homework... Oh yeah! I'm on it—mostly. I will be—soon."

She sighs and asks about Tilly.

"Who?" I reply.

She gives me the side-eye before she continues. "Fancy, think carefully about—"

"—I don't have time for introspection."

"Do you have time for an existential crisis? I think you're having one right now."

I shrug and make my way to the door. "This is my chance to be popular and get the guy. It turns out the guy sucks. But I can still get to the level of popularity I've longed for. This is my shot and I'm gonna take it."

CHAPTER 11

Whatever joy I thought I would feel rubbing Rahim in everyone's faces is actually multiplied by a thousand! We were holding hands outside the school and could hear students asking each other, *How did she get him? What does he see in her? How long has this been going on?* Some students asked how we met, and I told them about our perfect meet-cute. And then I smiled, like it was no big deal that I'm dating the hot guy.

But the best part happened just a few minutes ago, when Rahim walked me to my locker. Guess who was there—Tilly! Her eyes grew to ten times their normal size. Her mouth formed a perfect O, and I swear she stopped breathing. I leaned in and hugged Rahim, and he hugged me back. We then sweetly said our goodbyes. It was exactly like in a romance book. Finally, I'm not the chubby, sassy sidekick. I'm the heroine!

Tilly followed Rahim with her eyes until he turned down the hall and was no longer visible. And then she looked back to me and waited for me to explain. The fact is I really wanted to. I wanted to tell her everything. But here's the thing about being petty—you have to go in all the way. So even though I miss her and longed to tell her what's been going on, I couldn't.

Finally, Tilly blurted out, "What was that?"

"Oh, that? Just Rahim hugging me, again. He loves public displays of affection. You just missed us kissing. Well, gotta go! See you at the party!"

Imani and her crew of jackals have been eyeing me all day. If looks could kill, I would not be here right now, and I'm not the only one getting some heat.

I see Rahim and his friends head to the locker room and hear my name come up. I hold the door open just a little after they enter. It's a risky move, but I really want to know what they're saying and, more importantly, what Rahim tells them.

I overhear one guy, whose name I don't know, ask Rahim if he is going out with me because I'm willing to go all the way, or close to it. I want to run in there and tell the guy off, but I wait and see what Rahim says in return.

"Nah, it's not like that," Rahim replies.

"Then what's it like?" the guy asks.

"I don't know, man. She's...smart. She reads—a lot. Maybe too much." He groans.

I poke my head in a little farther, trying to get a good look. The guy starts to ask another question, but Rahim walks off before he can finish.

Well, I guess that's better than nothing, right? He could have lied and said we were doing it or something sleazy like that. But it would have been nice if he'd talked about me with more passion and enthusiasm. I want him to appear utterly taken with me. Well, given the fact that we pretty much can't stand each other, I guess this is as good as it's going to get.

"Can I help you?" Coach Farr asks from a few feet away. I swallow hard and close the locker room door. I can't believe I didn't hear him coming down the hallway.

"Coach Farr, hi!"

"What are you doing looking inside the boys' locker room?"

"I, ah...I lost my earring and thought it rolled over this way, but I guess I was wrong. Sorry."

"You're not wearing any earrings," he points out.

Great, I get caught by Sherlock freaking Holmes!

"That's because I lost both. One this morning and one now. Oh well. Guess I wasn't meant to have them. Bye!" I reply, practically running down the hall. I am so busy running from what's behind me that I pay no attention to the person I crash into.

"Hey, watch where you're going!" someone says. I look up and find myself face to face with the guy who threw the bag of Doritos at my feet back at CVS—Tyson.

Tyson is hot; I can't deny that. He's much taller than Rahim. He wears a clean-cut low fade and a disarming smile. What puts Tyson over the top and gets him a ton of girls are his dimples. They just make the girls melt. And he knows it.

"Sorry about that," I say, not stopping to chat.

"Wait, hang on! You the girl that's hooking up with my boy Rahim, right?"

"No. I'm the young lady that Rahim has the good fortune to be dating," I correct him.

He holds his hands up, palms out, letting me know he surrenders. "Okay, my bad. Are you that Voodoo witch chick? Why my boy dating you?"

"Isn't it obvious? I obtained a vial of his blood and now he has to do what I say," I reply, not bothering to hide my irritation.

"Yo! For real?" He takes one look at the scowl on my face and says, "Yeah, yeah. You got jokes. Seriously, what's up with the two of you? Rahim and me, we been boys forever. He never said anything about you two."

"Sounds like your issue is with him."

"He not here right now, so I'm asking you. So . . . what's up with you two? Is it serious? I'm sayin', when did this happen?"

"I don't want to be rude, but it's been a long week and I'm on the precipice."

"Precipice? Okay, shorty, come through with the big words. I see you."

"I'm not short!" I remind him.

"Okay, sorry. Look, I heard about this guy who went to Haiti and fell in love with some woman over there. He started cheating on her, and you know what she did? One morning he woke up and found a black chicken on his doorstep. Later that night, he came out the shower, saw himself in the mirror, and his *thing* shrank to the size of a grape! Is that true? Can you Voodoo chicks really do that?"

I should go the mature route, but this is too good a chance to pass up. "We can. In fact..." I look down at his crotch area. "I just did."

"Yeah, right! You playin'," he says with a smug, know-it-all smile.

It takes everything in me not to crack up laughing. In the end, I hold my serious demeanor. "*Am* I playing, Tyson? Or is it shrinking as we speak?"

The smug smile on Tyson's face disappears. I watch as panic fills his eyes when I look at his crotch again. He looks down at me, and I give him by best devious smile. His eyes widen with fear. He starts running down the hall, passing Coach Farr.

"Tyson, where you going in such a hurry?"

He yells back, "I gotta check something, Coach!"

119

At lunch, I sit by myself in my little corner. It's only when Rahim comes to get me that I remember that we should sit together. I didn't think about the lunch part! As we make our way to his table, I see Tilly in the corner of my eye. She looks confused, like she woke up in the wrong movie. But me, I'm finally in the rom-com I always wanted.

I get to be at the same table as the basketball team. They are a loud bunch, but I can't lie, they always seem to be having fun. Almost all of the guys have girlfriends at the table with them. Many of them are also on teams. There are three girls I remember seeing on the track team and two who are on the swim team.

When Rahim and I sit down, the first person to acknowledge me is Tyson. He towers above me. I expect him to be mad and ready to tell me off. I watch as his serious expression morphs into a smile. "I was salty at first, but yeah, you got me! I ain't no punk. I can admit, you got me good." Instead of being cursed out, I am rewarded with a fist bump. Rahim asks what that was all about, and I recount the story.

The rest of lunch goes by even better than I could have dreamed. It isn't even the fact that everyone is still whispering about us; it's how easy and laid-back Rahim's friends are. The group jokes around, while Tyson drones on about his dream of becoming a music supervisor for a hit TV show. He complains that most supervisors suck at selecting the right song to play during pivotal scenes.

"There's a science to it, man. You don't just play any old song. There's a method," he adds passionately. I was quick to dismiss him at first, but the more he talks the more sense he makes. He'd actually make a really good music supervisor.

While Tyson goes on and on, Rahim remains mostly quiet and a little distant. I text him although he's sitting right next to me.

> **ME:** Can you at least act like you are at the table with me? We have to really sell this.

> **RAHIM:** What do you want me to do, take you right here at the table? Is that what they do in the dumb romance books you read?

> **ME:** What is your problem?

> **RAHIM:** How do I know that you can really make this potion? What if you are just playing me, like you did to Tyson?

> **ME:** I'm not.

> **RAHIM:** How do I know?

> **ME:** You don't. It's called trust.

Imani enters the lunchroom and says something to her band of merry minions. They nod and laugh. And then she comes over to our table.

"Hi, Rahim. Been a while. You good?" she asks as she literally wedges herself right between us. Does this girl have nerve or what? "Oh, Fancy, you don't mind, do you? There's something I need to talk to Rahim about," she says. Before I can reply, she's already whispering into his ear.

ARGH!

I will not give her the satisfaction of knowing that her actions have gotten to me. I just smile at her, say, "Sure, no worries," and take a bite of my burger. But all I taste is the bitterness and fury that comes with watching a girl blatantly try to steal my fake boyfriend.

Tyson says, "Go easy, Imani. Fancy don't play. She got that black magic thing on lock. She put a spell on my boy right here, right?" he jokes, and playfully punches Rahim on his shoulder.

Imani replies, "I'm not afraid of Fancy. But now I get why you two are together. You threatened him with some Voodoo 'desperation powder'? That's the only way this thing makes sense. You're not Rahim's type."

I refuse to give her the satisfaction of seeing me upset. I turn my back to her and face Tyson. That way, she knows that I don't care enough to even watch her antics. I lean over and whisper to Tyson, "How much prison time do you get for murder if you're under eighteen?"

He laughs. "You my people, for real. And I can be your alibi. We were hanging out all night, your honor."

I smile despite myself.

Unlike me, Tyson has a perfect view of what Imani and

Rahim are doing. And whatever it is, it puts Tyson on high alert. I turn around and see Imani shamelessly stroking his arm!

I'm fuming, and Imani knows it. She gets up and says, "I'm gonna go—let's catch up later, okay, Rah?" He nods. Imani walks away, making sure to take her time so Rahim and the other guys can watch her seductive walk.

"*Rah*, can I see you out in the hallway for a second?" I ask, barely able to hide my irritation.

He rolls his eyes. "I didn't finish eating yet."

I glare at him. He reluctantly follows me out to the hallway.

"Why are you trying to embarrass me?" I demand.

"What?"

"What'll everyone think when they see you and Imani together? She was all over you!"

"You care a lot about what everyone thinks," he accuses.

"And you don't?"

He shrugs. "It's whatever."

"Oh, really?" I look down at his Jordans. It's a different pair from the ones he was wearing the night before. These are black-and-white suede with striped laces. I have never seen him wear shoes that weren't impeccably clean and fresh. I swear he must spend hours tending to them. "So you don't care what people think—that means I can step on your shoes and you won't care that they get dirty? Because it's whatever, right?"

"That's different."

"No, it's not! My reputation is just as important as your stupid shoes!"

"They aren't shoes. They're Jordans. And don't you even think about stepping on them."

"Oh, so you do care if someone sees you with scuffed-up sneakers?"

"That's not it. These aren't cheap. I can't just let you put dirt on them."

"No, but you can put dirt on my name?" I ask.

"When did I do that?"

"ARGH! You let Imani grope you. That tells everyone that my boyfriend doesn't respect me. You're throwing metaphorical dirt on my name!"

The two of us start speaking at once. We're too busy arguing to notice that someone has entered the hallway—Mrs. Washington.

Damn.

"So how is the new couple doing?" she asks, staring hard at me.

I put my head on Rahim's shoulder. "We're great! Couldn't be better!"

"Uh-huh," she replies. "Rahim, give us a minute."

He takes off and goes back to the lunchroom.

"Mrs. Washington—"

"Stop! Stop right there. The only thing I want to hear from you is that you're working on all the assignments you owe. If you don't meet this deadline, I'll call your parents. Am I making myself absolutely clear?"

"Yes," I mutter, shifting my weight from one foot to the other.

"What was that song you told me about a kid who got sent back to Haiti?"

I reply, " 'The Ballad of Jean-Louis.' "

"Well, pay attention, Fancy. Because the tune you're humming sounds very much like a ballad. . . ."

The last bell rings and everyone pours out of class. The feeling of freedom that comes with Friday is in the air. I overhear chatter about some guys on basketball team throwing an impromptu house party. I'm guessing Rahim is still mad and won't ask me to come along. That's just as well; I really need to work on all the assignments I owe this weekend. And I think we've faked it enough for today.

I see Rahim coming out of the school. When our eyes meet, he looks away. That stings a little. But true to his word, he makes it over to me, exactly what a boyfriend would do. I can tell by the look on his face that he's dreading being here with me.

"There's a party—" he begins.

"It's fine. You don't have to invite me. I'm behind on some stuff, so I'll be home studying," I reply.

He shrugs. "I can't go anyway. I have to take my little sister to her first music lesson today. It's all she can talk about."

"Oh, yeah, I forgot. You have a sister."

"Five of them. I'm surrounded by girls," he gripes.

"You don't have to say that like it's a bad—" The words die in my mouth as Tilly approaches us.

"Hi," she says.

"Oh. Hey," I reply awkwardly.

She looks at Rahim, waiting for an introduction, I guess.

"Rahim, this is Tilly, my best— We're in some of the same classes. Tilly, this is Rahim—my boyfriend."

Tilly's face falls slightly; she says hello and asks me if we can talk privately. I tell her that Rahim and I keep no secrets from each other. She can talk in front of him. Rahim looks uncomfortable being put on the spot.

"I was cleaning out my closet, and I found some of the stuff we used to play with back when... Anyway, here." Tilly hands me a small pouch.

"Oh, yeah. Thanks," I reply, shoving it into my coat pocket.

"So... how are you?" she asks uneasily.

Before I can reply, Jason comes up and playfully covers her eyes from behind.

"I thought your school had some kind of event and you couldn't walk me home today," Tilly says.

"I decided to skip it. I thought we'd try a new restaurant I heard about. They have the best vegan hot dogs, and they toast the bun with soy butter."

I laugh without meaning to. The thought that Tilly would enjoy a hot dog with no meat is just too much. She and I have put away racks of ribs faster than most adults! And now... I wish she would just come out and tell him who she really is. How can he like her if she's faking it?

Really, Fancy?

Yeah, yeah, but that's different. I mean, I *know* I'm faking it, and so does Rahim. But Tilly and Jason . . .

"Why are you laughing?" she demands.

"Nothing. I just forgot how much you love vegan hot dogs," I reply, rolling my eyes.

"Well, it just so happens I do! I love them!" she snaps. "Let's go!"

Before she can step away, I shout, "I'm excited, too. Rahim just invited me to hang out with him and his friends—well, our friends. We should get going!" I take Rahim's hand.

I'm grateful when he doesn't question it and just goes along. We walk down the block, and I try not to look back. I'm worried that if I do, I'll see that Tilly doesn't even care that I'm walking away. I'm also worried she does care and I hurt her feelings. There's just no way to win right now.

When we turn the corner, I thank him for going along with me. He asks about the tension between Tilly and me. I tell him I don't want to talk about it.

"Okay, fine. I guess. But I really do need to pick up my sister for her music lesson. You can come with me if you want. It's just up the street."

"I don't want Tilly and Jason to see me alone. So . . . yeah, I guess."

We walk up to a small two-story building with a banner that reads, AS WE GROW LEARNING CENTER. The window is decorated with cutouts of kid handprints, bright leaves, and colorful art projects.

"Wait right here, I'll get Asia," Rahim says. He comes back a few minutes later with the cutest four-year-old I've ever seen. She's wearing a puffy pink cloud coat, and her Afro is in a neat ponytail. She has her brother's eyes, and freckles on the bridge of her nose.

"Hi!" she says as soon as she makes it out the door and sees me.

"Hi! It's nice to meet you. I'm Fancy. I love your coat. Pink is so pretty!"

She beams and turns around in a full circle so that I can appreciate her coat in all its splendor.

Asia turns her attention back to me as we start walking. "Today is my first music lesson! I'm gonna do good! I'm gonna be bestest best!"

I laugh. "I like your confidence. I think you'll be really good, too."

"Why do they call you Fancy?" she asks.

I don't get a chance to reply because by then Asia has already moved on to her next question.

"Are you Rah's girlfriend?" she says with a mischievous grin. "Ah…"

Rahim rescues me. "Enough with the questions, okay?"

"Dad said there's no such thing as too many questions," she says in a serious tone that makes me smile.

"That's true, but maybe hold them for later," Rahim suggests.

"Okay," she says, sounding disappointed.

"Can I ask *you* some questions, Asia?" I ask.

"Yes!" she replies, only too happy to talk about herself. I ask her about her favorite ice cream flavor, sleepover game, and book. She goes on and on, with no end in sight. Rahim mouths, *I'm sorry,* because his little sister is talking a mile a minute. I wave him off, letting him know I'm more than happy to talk to my new friend.

We're having a very serious debate over which ice cream flavor is the best: strawberry versus chocolate. I don't expect Rahim to join in, but he does. He wants to stick up for the flavor he thinks is best—vanilla!

"No!" Asia and I shout at the same time.

Then things get really rowdy. We all begin speaking at once, vigorously defending our preferences. But in the end, we're both outmatched by Asia. She simply says, "I'm right. And everyone else is wrong. I win!"

Rahim gets a text and furrows his brow.

"What's wrong?" I ask.

"It's from Asia's music school. The teacher has the flu and won't be coming in today."

"No music?" Asia asks, sounding distraught.

Rahim kneels down so that the two of them are at eye level. "I'm sorry, Lil Bit. It looks like your first class isn't gonna happen today."

"No!" She pouts and stamps her foot.

"What did I tell you about having a tantrum when you don't get what you want?" Rahim says with authority.

"No!" Asia replies.

"What did I tell you?"

She grumbles, "You said that I have to do my best to make something bad turn to something good."

"That's right. So, music class is canceled—how you gonna handle that? How do you make it better?"

She turns her eyes toward the sky as if she's waiting for some celestial guidance. And then she looks at me and says, "We can go for ice cream!"

He laughs. "Okay, I should've seen that one coming. Come here, you little scam artist," he says, playfully wrestling with his sister. He tickles her, and she cracks up laughing. Rahim gets up and takes her hand. "Isn't it too cold for ice cream?" he asks.

Asia and I yell, "No!"

Rahim is taken aback. "Okay, okay! I'm outnumbered."

"I'm glad we're getting ice cream. But my heart is broken," she says as she hugs me ever so dramatically. Both Rahim and I suppress a smile. This kid is too much.

We start walking once again. I ask Asia what instrument she's going to be learning, and she says piano. I stop.

"What is it?" Rahim asks.

"Asia was going to go for her first piano lesson today?"

"Yeah. Why?" he asks.

"I think I have an idea, but first, do you know where we can get Tupperware around here?"

I knock on Ms. Dorcy's door, Asia and Rahim standing beside me. She reacts pretty much the way I thought she would.

"Who the hell is at my door?" she shouts.

"It's me—Fancy."

"The one with the odd name," she replies, still unwilling to open the door.

"Yes. I have a sweet kid here with me. Her name is Asia. She needs a piano lesson."

"No. Go away."

"Okay. I guess I'll get going," I reply. Rahim looks at me, confused. I signal for him to hold on. "It's too bad, though, Ms. Dorcy. I found this really nice Tupperware set—ten pieces. I wanted to give them to you as a thank-you gift, but—"

The door flies open. "Are they the good kind?" she says. "I don't take no imitation."

I hand them over. She studies them and nods, letting me know she approves. She takes a look at Asia and Rahim. And then back at me.

"Fine. One lesson," she says.

Asia looks at Ms. Dorcy with suspicion. It's fitting, since

Ms. Dorcy is looking at her the very same way. They both have their arms folded stubbornly across their chests. They both pout and glare at the other. It's their "high noon" moment. They're actually waiting to see who blinks first.

"Asia, say hi to Ms. Dorcy and thank her for agreeing to give you a lesson," Rahim says, trying to gently guide his sister into Ms. Dorcy's apartment.

She mumbles something that sounds somewhat like what her brother asked her to say. But all the while, she stands perfectly still. She wants us to know that while we can take her here, we can't force her to cooperate.

"You really want to learn piano? Or is this just something to do when the cartoons go to commercial?" Ms. Dorcy asks.

"No, I want to learn to play!" Asia says proudly.

"I don't think you do," Ms. Dorcy counters dismissively.

"Yes, I do," Asia insists as she stamps her foot.

"No, you don't!" Ms. Dorcy says, stamping her foot just like Asia did.

"Yes, I do!" Asia screams at the top of her lungs.

"Well then..." Ms. Dorcy opens her door wide. "You better come in and show me."

Asia, feeling like she has something to prove, enters the apartment. Ms. Dorcy gives us a knowing smile as we start to follow them in. However, before we can get past the threshold, she stops us.

"All parents and relatives stay outside," she says.

"But we—"

"No family allowed. Kids can't focus. You two stay out in the hallway until we're done."

She signals for us to hold on and comes back to the door with two glasses of soda.

"Here," she says, handing the glasses over to us. "Now, we'll be done in half an hour. You two stay here and don't make out. This is a hallway. Not a brothel."

Rahim and I look at each other, not sure if Ms. Dorcy is joking or not. "Asia, we'll be out here when you're ready, okay?" Rahim calls out.

"Okay! This piano is so big! I like it!" Asia shouts just as Ms. Dorcy closes the door in our faces.

Rahim looks concerned. "Will she be okay?"

"Taste your soda. Does it have any fizz?" I ask.

He takes a sip. "Yeah, it's carbonated. Why?"

"It means she likes you. Ms. Dorcy doesn't hand out fizz to just anyone." He looks at me, confused. I shrug. "She's an old lady who is serious about soda carbonation and plasticware ownership."

We hear a scale being played on the piano inside. We hear Ms. Dorcy telling Asia to watch her posture and to relax her shoulders. I motion for us to walk a few yards away.

"Listen, thanks for helping us. Lil Bit's a handful. And she's had a hard year," he confesses.

"Oh, I'm sorry. Why has it been so hard?"

He looks away and shrugs. "You know. Stuff. Anyway, thanks again."

"No problem."

Rahim clears his throat and rubs the back of his neck, still looking off to the side. "Yeah, there's something else...," he adds.

"What is it?"

"I said that I would go along with this fake boyfriend thing, and...well, I shouldn't have let Imani...That was my bad."

"Ah...thanks," I reply.

"I know you said that you didn't want to talk about it, but what's up with you and that Tilly chick? Why all the drama?"

I start to tell him, and I'm taken aback by how easy it is to talk to him. He doesn't interrupt me or judge what I'm saying. He just listens.

"...I'm pretty sure our friendship is over," I conclude. "And that's crazy, because who wouldn't want to be my friend? I mean, I'm kind of amazing," I joke. He says nothing.

"Rahim, this is the part where you disagree with me."

"About your being amazing? I didn't hear anything I disagreed with." It's not his words that get me; but the sincerity behind them.

Okay fine, I hate him three percent less.

Maybe four...

CHAPTER 12

I am dreaming about what happened Friday—my moment with Rahim in the hallway of Ms. Dorcy's apartment—when my alarm goes off. How is it already Monday? Where did the weekend go? It doesn't matter. The point is I get to be Rahim's girlfriend. And in just three weeks, we'll attend Imani's party together. I don't think life could be any more perfect. Before I get in the shower, I receive an email from Mrs. Washington reminding me that I'm running out of time to get all my work in. I'm not worried. I have it all under control.

When I get to school, Rahim is waiting for me. We find ourselves gazing at each other and holding hands as we make our way down the halls. We don't even look to see if Imani is around or not. This isn't about her anymore—well, not *just* about her. The day goes by in a haze, and out of all the lessons we learn in class, the only thing I retain is how good it feels to have Rahim holding my hand. Later, when school lets out, he's outside my last class. He invites me to Tyson's house with the rest of the group to play video games. I need a school-related reason for staying out, so I text my mom and tell her I'm taking a pre-SAT class after school.

On our way to his house, Tyson keeps bragging about his *Mario Kart* skills and how no one on the team can beat him. He's right—no one on the team can. But I hadn't been on the team....

Who knew I'd be so good at that game?

Tyson is so hurt, he refuses to talk to me afterward. And he accuses Rahim of bringing in a ringer. Rahim brags about me the rest of the day. It makes me blush and grin like a fool.

The next day, Tyson is still in his feelings and doesn't want to hang out with us. It takes six hot wings; chili fries, and a large Mountain Dew to make peace. On Thursday some of the girls from the basketball team ask the guys for a polite, friendly game after school. When Rahim sees me cheering for the girls, he places a hand on his heart and pretends to be gravely wounded.

"I thought we had something," he teases.

I shrug. "Sorry, I'm a Black girl. That means I'm contractually obligated to do two things: root for other Black girls and point out bad weaves in Tyler Perry films."

He says he feels betrayed. I ask what would make him feel better, especially since they lost the game. He informs me that nothing will heal his broken heart except the "Wing and Fries" apology I gave to Tyson. I laugh and get him the food. He shares it with me and hardly breaks eye contact as we eat.

On our way back, Rahim asks how things are going with Tilly. He seems disappointed when I don't have an update.

"I just think you two should figure something out. I mean, that's your girl, right?" he asks.

"It's complicated." Talking about Tilly feels like digging into a wound that hasn't even healed yet. I change the subject. "Tyson said you guys have a new coach. How's it going?"

"He's okay, but Coach Grayson was better. He made us work harder. He's the reason we got to finals last year." It's hard to miss the admiration in his voice.

"What happened to Coach Grayson?"

"His wife got some fancy job and they had to move," he replies bitterly. "How long until my potion is ready?"

My heart sinks. For a moment I'd forgotten about our agreement. I let myself believe this thing with us was real. But it's not. It's an arrangement. If I don't get him a potion, will that be the end of everything?

"Fancy? The potion. How's it going?"

"Great! Just…great."

Okay, that's a lie, but I've been gathering the items I need—the real ones. No more substitutions. So, I'm sure it'll go well from this point on. The only thing I'm having trouble getting is fresh goat's blood. The last time I tried, I used frozen. But every butcher I go to is always out of goat. There's one more butcher shop on my list. If they don't have any, I'm screwed.

When I wake up Friday morning, I check my Insta. Everyone on my feed is already showing off their outfit options for Imani's party, even though we're still two weeks out. I'm getting a little discouraged. I can't seem to find anything grand enough for the party. When I find something I like, it's too expensive or they don't have my size. I scroll down and see the wide array of dresses everyone is planning on wearing. Their outfits are beautiful! There's no doubt about it—my dress needs to be next level. The more I scroll, the worse I feel. Suddenly, an ad catches my eye. I click the link and just like that…I've found it!

I exhale in the most dramatic but appropriate fashion. It's everything I was looking for and more. It's the ultimate dress, and they have my size! It's about fifty bucks more than I have, but I'll figure out a way to make up the difference. I have two perfectly good kidneys, and I only need one. So, it's decided. I'm getting this dress! I put it in my virtual cart. "I'll be back for you, my love," I promise my new gown.

My cell dings and a reminder pops up: Homework due! Damn it! I'm supposed to hand all my stuff in today! I spring out of bed, get dressed, and rush out of the house. I make it to school just in time. I take a beat and prepare for whatever horrors are headed my way. Is there any excuse I can make up that Mrs. Washington will buy?

How much does it cost to get a whole new identity? Does the US have an extradition treaty with Switzerland? They have really good cheese and the best chocolate.

Sigh. It's too late to plan my escape anyway. I'm here. There's a note posted on her door: MRS. WASHINGTON IS OFFSITE AND WILL BE BACK MONDAY.

Yes, thank You, White Jesus!

That gives me a whole weekend to try and catch up. I think I can convince Mrs. Washington to move away from the nuclear option of calling my parents if I come in Monday with at least some of the work. I'll gladly do all the detention she wants if we can avoid that step. No matter what happens, I'll be home, working my butt off all weekend.

Later, when school is over, Rahim asks if I can join them at the skate park. I consider saying no, given my new resolve to get my work done this weekend. But then it hits me—technically Friday isn't part of the weekend. It's a *precursor* to the weekend. So I agree to go along. But on our way to the park, Rahim changes his mind and asks if we can do our own thing.

Um, yes please . . .

We split off from the group and wait for the light so we can cross. A city bus pulls over and lets the passengers out. We wait silently, hand in hand. This doesn't feel like something that's too good to be true anymore. It feels real. I smile to myself.

"What's up with that grin?" he asks. He looks over at the bus. It features an ad for a travel site. There's a cute couple having a candlelit dinner in a hotel, with the Eiffel Tower in the background.

"Oh, I get it. You're daydreaming about Paris because of the poster? Let me guess, you think it's the most romantic place on earth, right?"

"I don't think that about Paris."

He places his hand over his chest and gasps, like he's suddenly in a state of shock. I playfully poke him with my elbow. He laughs at me. I'm forced to explain myself.

"Yes, Paris is a 'go to' for romance and it's 'Fancy approved.' But it's not the *most* romantic place."

"Okay, my bad. So . . . where is the most romantic place on earth?"

"For me . . . the New York Public Library! The main branch in Manhattan."

When he finally stops laughing, he realizes that I'm not joking. "Wait, for real? That's your idea of romance? A library?!"

"It's not just a library. It's *the* library. It's one of the most prestigious institutions in America. Its marble floors and hand-painted ceilings are a thing of beauty. The Rose Reading Room alone has been visited by dozens of literary greats and Nobel prizewinners. And for your information, it has over six times as much marble as the New York Stock Exchange. It's been recognized and designated as one of NYC's most impressive landmarks. And it's protected by two ferocious stone lions called Patience and Fortitude."

"You know the names of the lions?"

"Yeah. That's what I called the two pet goldfish I had a few years back."

"Every time I think you can't be any more odd..."

"Imagine standing in the middle of a place that is home to more than twenty million books? That's basically like being in the nexus of the universe," I inform him.

"The nexus of the universe, huh?" he says doubtfully.

"Yes! And what about their grand staircase? Oh man, that's where romance lives."

"On the staircase?"

"Grand staircase. Thank you."

He smiles and says, "You know what, I kind of get it—wanting to feel like a part of something really big. I'll show you my secret universe sometime."

"Should I be afraid?" I ask.

"Nah. Whatever you're thinking, that's not it. I'm not just some guy with a love of sneakers. I'm full of surprises."

"Oh, so what is it?" I push.

"No, not telling. You have to wait and see. Yo, I'm starving!" he says.

"There's nothing in our deal that says I have to feed you," I reply.

"That's cold, man!"

I laugh. "Fine. We can go eat. But it's on you," I reply.

"And what am I getting in exchange for paying?"

"The pleasure of my company," I say proudly.

He thinks about it for a beat and then says, "That's a fair trade."

We walk down Church Avenue, past a row of restaurants. It's late, and most of them have closed. The only one that's open is a small hole-in-the-wall place called Island Pot.

"Have you ever been here before?" I ask.

"No. They make Haitian food?"

"Yeah. It's really good. You ever tried it?"

"Nah. But I'm up for it."

We enter the small island-themed restaurant. The space is warm and has a soft reddish glow to it. The woman behind the counter smiles and greets us. Her Haitian accent is unmistakable to me.

"Hello, I'm Gladys. Welcome to Island Pot. What can I get you?"

"Ah, I don't know. I've never had Haitian food before," Rahim says.

"It's okay, I've got you covered," I reply.

I order the most traditional Haitian meal on the menu—rice and beans with fried crispy pork and salad. When the food arrives, Rahim reaches for one of the condiment jars on the table. I stop him.

"That's called pikliz. It's really spicy."

"I can handle it," he says with certainty.

"No, I don't think you can."

He heaps a pile of pikliz on top of the food and shoves it into his mouth. He looks happy as he chews and crunches away. But he soon encounters a pepper. Without warning, Rahim grabs the pitcher of ice water on the table and gulps down nearly half of it. I'm laughing so hard I can't catch my breath.

"I told you it was hot!" I remind him.

"I can't feel my lips."

I politely ask Gladys to bring out something that'll help Rahim. She comes out of the kitchen and places a small bowl of ice cream at the center of our table.

"It's called cream cocoye—coconut ice cream," I explain.

He picks up a spoon and digs into it. He brings the first spoonful to my lips. "Here, you first—in case Gladys is trying to poison me." I open my mouth, and he actually goes through with it—he feeds me ice cream!

He leans in and kisses me.

It feels like I'm in flight. There's just no other way to put it.

Fancy, do not let one—albeit exhilarating—kiss make you jump to conclusions.

What should we wear for senior prom? Should we go with matching outfits? Or is that too cutesy? Are summer weddings still a thing? Or should we do winter wonderland?

"White Jesus, have You ever felt like You were in a moment that was so beautiful, so perfect, it couldn't possibly belong to You? That's exactly how I felt last night. Getting my first kiss was mind-blowing, and having Rahim be the one to give me that kiss? C'mon, that can't be real, right?"

WJ nods.

"But it was real. It wasn't a book, or film, or some elaborate daydream. The only thing that could have made it better would have been having Tilly to talk to about it. She'd ask a million questions, we'd go over every second leading up to the kiss. I miss her."

White Jesus shakes His head, disappointed.

"I know, You think I should reach out. And it's not like I don't miss her. I saw a hearse go by yesterday that had a gorgeous silver trim. Tilly would have loved that.

"I should call. But what if she doesn't miss me? What if our friendship is all but forgotten? I don't want to be the stray fry left at the bottom of the McDonald's bag. It's Saturday, she's probably at the craft store, plotting her next dollhouse masterpiece."

I pick up my cell to call her, but I put it back down. I don't know how I'll take it if she sends me to voicemail.

My mom enters my room and tells me to get ready for Saturday morning service. I'd love to ask her if I could skip it, but she's still upset with me for buying the outfit I wore to meet Rahim. I can't risk adding to her wrath, so I get ready.

"Did you do your homework last night, so you can have the rest of today free?" she asks.

"Free to go to more church services? Clean my room? Mop the floors? What amazing adventure awaits me?" I reply sarcastically.

"Don't you remember? I'm off this afternoon."

That's when I remember the podcast we are overdue to listen to together. "Oh yeah! I forgot. Murder! Copy that," I reply. She beams and walks out of my room.

I was going to turn her down, but she looked really excited. And it's only a few hours long. I should be back in my room and at my desk working before nightfall. "Yeah, I got this."

Murder really is the best way to relax after church. We listen to the latest episode of the *My Fair Murder* podcast, twice, stopping each time right before the killer is revealed to go over our notes. We review the case as if our lives depend on it.

"Mom, there is no way a woman who is barely one hundred and twenty pounds can drag a body that far without help! I'm telling you, the neighbor is in on it!" I plead.

Mom jumps up and proclaims, "No! She just used the neighbor to access his storage unit. She's controlling this whole thing!" We go back and forth, each of us eager to prove our point.

"Hey, no shouting!" Dad says, standing in the entryway. This isn't the first time he's had to come to the living room and ask us to be quieter. It's not even the second time. He looks around and furrows his brow. The living room is in a rare state of disorder. There are bags of half-eaten snacks, the remnants of a large pepperoni pizza, and empty soda cans.

"I thought you two were going to keep it down," Dad says.

We both start talking at once. He holds his hand up and reminds us about the last time he took sides. Mom made him sleep on the sofa. It was a mess. So we have a rule: Neither of us is allowed to drag poor Dad into our cases.

"Okay, okay," Mom says, resigned. I nod and promise that we won't ask him to pick a side and that we'll keep it down.

"I'm glad you two are almost done. This is the last episode, right? That's what I heard you say this morning." Dad is hoping for some peace in the house.

"It's the last of this podcast, but there's a whole new season of *Murder & Money & Mayhem*," Mom says. We both cheer as my dad groans.

"Sweetheart, I saw a lot of people coming and going from Mr. Henderson's yard. I think he's having a yard sale today."

Dad's eyes light up. Mom and I exchange a look. It only takes seconds for Dad to fly out of the house and seek new "treasure."

Mom calls after him: "Only one thing. Please! Just get one thing!"

"Mom, don't play the end of the episode yet. I'm gonna make some more popcorn."

"Okay, I'll heat up the wings," Mom says, following me to the kitchen.

While we ready another wave of junk food, she asks about Tilly. "I haven't seen her in a few weeks. Is she okay?"

Yeah, she's great! She has Jason. But that's fine because I have Rahim. It's not like we have to be friends forever. That's just something people say. It rarely works out that way.

I keep my thoughts to myself, but out loud I reply, "She's got stuff to do, I guess."

Mom looks me over. I hate how well she knows me. "Is everything okay?" she asks.

"Yup!" I shrug. Her expression tells me she's not convinced. "We've been doing different stuff lately—without each other."

"Okay, but don't forget she's your best friend."

I don't think that's true anymore, but I don't want to talk about it. I can't trust myself not to tear up. I actually want to talk about something else: boys. It's tricky with Haitian moms. The subject of boys can lead to an open and honest conversation or get you sent to a convent. It's basically a roll of the dice.

"Mom, when you met Dad back in Haiti, how did you know you liked him? I mean, really liked him?" I ask, holding my breath.

"Fancy, do you—"

"No, I don't have a boyfriend and I'm not doing anything. I just . . . wanted to ask. How did you know that he was the one?"

She shrugs. "My mother told me he was."

"That's it?"

"Yes. He was from a good family; they own a little bit of land. So she told me he was the boy for me. And he was."

"If Grandma hadn't picked him for you, would you have picked him on your own?"

"No. He had skinny legs," she says in all seriousness.

"Mom!"

She cracks a smile and says, "I found something I liked about him eventually. And after some time, I fell in love. And we are very happy together. But your father, he knows if I ever get the chance, I'll leave him for Obama."

I laugh but I know she's only half joking. "How did you know Dad liked you? Was it the way he looked at you?"

"No, it was the way he couldn't *stop* looking at me...."

I flash back to Rahim and the way he tends to gaze at me. Please, let this be about more than just a potion or a party....

CHAPTER
13

My dad takes my mom out for dinner Sunday night. I use that time to finally crack open a book. I swear the words all blend together to form a cutout of Rahim. He's smiling at me from the pages of my history book. He's even sexy with words written on his face! I think about the kiss again, and my face grows warm.

"Hello?" Rahim says.

I don't even remember picking up my cell, but I guess I did. The next thing I know, the two of us are on the phone for over an hour. He tells me that his dad is working late and his sisters are at a concert. Asia was too young to go, so he's stuck baby-sitting her. She fell asleep in front of the TV, rewatching the newest version of *The Little Mermaid* for the millionth time. He asks if I want to come over, he has something to show me. I'm out the door and on the bus in no time.

When I get to Rahim's house, I see Asia sprawled out on the sofa, sucking her thumb. She's wearing a tiara, and I would expect nothing less. Rahim tells me she is now officially a student of Ms. Dorcy's and will start taking piano lessons every week.

The house is cluttered with toys and dolls, all of which I'm sure belong to Asia. But given that seven people live here, it's pretty tidy.

"Let me take Lil Bit upstairs—be right back," he says.

He grabs his little sister and effortlessly hoists her onto his shoulders. She wakes up and grumbles, "No, I want Mommy to put me to bed!" She tries to wiggle and scoot out of his grasp. He puts her down on the stairs.

"You know she's not here," Rahim says.

"But I want her!" she snaps.

He holds her little face in his hand and says, "If you go to bed, we'll have a tea party tomorrow. Promise."

"Will you dress up like Daddy does? He wears a funny hat."

"No."

"Why not?" she demands.

"Asia, get your butt upstairs!"

I watch as tears spring to her eyes. Rahim's face softens. "Who's in charge of what Disney movies we see?"

"I am!" she says proudly.

"Do you want me to give that job to someone else?"

"No!"

"Then let's get upstairs before I give your very important job away."

"Okay," she mutters. He picks her up. She waves goodbye to me from over Rahim's shoulders. I wave in return. When he comes back down, he finds me looking at the photos on the wall.

"I love the family pics. When did you all go to Italy?" I ask, looking at the picture of them standing in front of the Milan Cathedral.

"About three years ago."

"Nice! Is this your mom? She's so pretty," I reply, pointing to a woman in a sundress standing in a photo by herself in front of a garden.

"Yeah, that's her," he says, sounding bitter.

"Is everything okay? You seemed a little...tense when Asia asked about your mom. Is she working a lot of overtime?"

"I don't know what she's doing," he snaps. I step back, not sure what I said to upset him. He sighs deeply and replies, "Sorry. My bad."

He takes my hand and we go down the hall to his room. His bedroom is clean-ish enough. There's a long line of sneakers near the foot of his bed—way too many. I can see the side of his closet; it's also filled with sneakers. Above the door there's a mini basketball hoop, and the top of his desk is filled with sports trophies.

"Look."

"What am I looking at?" I ask.

He points up toward the ceiling. Above us, there's an elaborate display of glow-in-the-dark decal stars and planets. They've been placed on wallpaper that depicts vast galaxies. I've seen stars stuck on walls before, but this is so much more intricate.

"My dad and I used to go to the Hayden Planetarium all the time when I was a kid. It was our favorite place. When I was little, I told him I wanted to take the stars and planets home with me. So, he came up with this. We constructed it together—little by little. It doesn't resemble our exact galaxy, of course, but it's a mix of all the stuff in space that we love. All the places we'd like to go."

"It's beautiful."

"It's better if I turn off the lights. Are you good with that?"

I look over at him. "Yeah, go ahead."

He flips the light switch off, and suddenly the entire galaxy is illuminated. The sheer amount of stars and planets radiating down on us is unreal. We lie down on the floor and look up at the wonder above.

"Do you show this to all the girls?"

"No girls are allowed in here, not even my sisters."

"Oh. So I'm your first...," I tease.

"Yeah, yeah. You're my first," he replies, playfully rolling his eyes.

"I can't get over how pretty it is."

"Oh, and check this out..." He holds up a small remote control and points it at the ceiling. Suddenly the cutout stars dim and twinkle in a random pattern. He points toward the moon. Every time he presses a button on the remote, it goes to a different phase.

"Basically, you are a god of your own universe?" I ask.

"Yeah, but I don't wanna brag."

I laugh. "Very mature of you."

"Not all of them are from our galaxy. When I was a kid, my dad would ask what planet I wanted to go to for that day. I always picked the planets that were the most adventurous and had a dangerous atmosphere. My dad would get all dressed up so we could 'go' there."

"Okay, so which planet did you want to go to the most and why?" I ask.

He points to an illustration on the far wall of a shiny, red-hot ball that floats against the night sky.

"That's it, right there. Planet 55 Cancri e," he says.

I scrunch my face at the red, blistering planet. It's a swirling orb inferno. "That planet looks like where the Devil goes to vacation."

He nods. "Well, I guess that fits—they call it 'The Hell Planet.'"

"I can see why."

"It takes Earth a year to go around the sun. But 55 Cancri e only takes about seventeen hours to go around theirs. That's how close they are to their sun. It's four thousand degrees on the planet. It has oceans made of lava and rains glass."

"Well, you can go if you want, but I think I'll stay here."

"Okay, cool. I'll have to haul the diamonds out myself."

"Diamonds?"

He nods his head slowly, wearing a knowing smile. "Yes. Because 55 Cancri e has a core that is made of pure diamonds."

"Can we go now? Beat the traffic?" I suggest. "How much do you think the diamonds are worth?"

"I looked it up once. It's about twenty nonillion. That's twenty with thirty zeros behind it," he explains.

I put my hand over my mouth. Rahim says, "Yeah, I know it's wild that that kind of money even exists."

"That's not what shocked me. I just realized that you—Rahim Robinson—are a complete nerd!"

He smiles. "Our secret?"

"Yeah, sure. I really should have paid more attention in class."

"It's cool. This section is a depiction of the planets that should not exist but do. That one over there, to the right, that's PSR B1620−26 b, commonly known as Methuselah. It's the oldest planet that's ever existed. But it shouldn't exist, because the stuff you need to make up a planet wasn't around then. And yet there it is."

"Hi, Methuselah!"

"That's what gave me the idea to ask you about making a potion. It defies logic. If a planet can do that, maybe a potion can, too."

I quickly change the subject, not wanting to dwell on the potion. "Hey, not to be too nosy, but...why did you get so upset before? Are you and your mom fighting? Are your parents fighting?"

He smiles, but there's no mistaking the sadness underneath. "They don't fight—not anymore. My mom took off."

"Oh...I'm sorry. I didn't know—"

"It's fine. I mean, it's not, but..." He shrugs.

I want to know what's going on, but it's clear pushing him would not be a good idea. We stay silent for a moment and then he says softly, "I love my mom, I do. And we all miss her, but she always seemed like she'd rather be somewhere other than here with us. When she left a year ago, none of us were surprised. But we didn't know how her leaving would affect my dad."

"Is he heartbroken? I know my dad would be if my mom left," I admit.

"It's more than that. It's like when she left, she took all the good parts of him with her. And now, we get this shell of a guy who...I don't even recognize."

"Maybe he just needs some time?" I offer gently.

"Fancy, my dad was always goofy and corny. He'd sing off-key in the car and embarrass us by hugging us in front of our friends. He'd come to my games and shout, 'That's my boy!' I would put my head down in embarrassment. But to be honest—I liked having him there.

"But ever since Mom left...he mostly sleeps and spaces out. That's why I need your potion. I need to give it to my dad so he'll stop loving and missing my mom. That way he can go back to who he used to be. Your potion can do that, right? Your potion can make my dad like he was before?"

"Yes."

Oh God, what did I just do?

Instead of heading home, I take the bus to the last butcher shop on my list. They are just about to close, so I quickly enter and get what I need. It isn't fun carrying goat in a bag on the bus. It wasn't a whole head or anything, just a few bony pieces, but I could have sworn all eyes were on me. I beat my parents back by only fifteen minutes or so. I wait until they go to bed and try once again to get the potion right.

I have everything set up, and this time I remember to put my braids in a high ponytail so there won't be another mishap. I double and triple check my list. I practice the chant under my breath. I have to get this right.

I put Rahim's dad's tie into the bowl along with all the other items. It's a real ceremony bowl I got from eBay. I light the match and chant my heart out. I recall how heartbroken Rahim was when he was talking about his dad, and I chant even louder. But the potion doesn't turn red. It doesn't even go dark brown like it did last time. The closest it gets is a light pink with gray undertones. I try mixing it two more times, but nothing! ARGH! I wonder if I can get the Voodoo owner to barter with me. He could give me the potion in exchange for something I have that he needs. The moment that thought comes to mind, I remember every story I've read where a dark mysterious figure offers to provide a magical mixture in exchange for something. It never turns out well. I could see it now: The store owner would say, "Yes, little girl, I have the potion, and all I need from you is—YOUR SOUL!!!"

I'm exhausted and deflated. I slump down on my bed.

I can't help but hear Rahim's voice and how crestfallen he was as he talked about his dad. I can picture how happy that home used to be before everything changed. There was so much desperation in Rahim's eyes. And I came in and made things worse. Damn. This Voodoo thing really did seem easier in the movies.

Maybe I can get Rahim to talk to his dad? No, I'm sure he's tried that before. And besides, he's already counting on me and my "magic" potion. *Wait!* I sit up suddenly and look over at White Jesus.

"I have an idea! Maybe I don't need to talk to Rahim. Maybe the person I need to talk to is his dad! Yes!"

I get online and find Mr. Robinson's Facebook page. I send him a direct message. I sure hope I'm not overstepping. But then again, I've already messed so many things up, what more could go wrong?

I burst into Mrs. Washington's office first thing the next
morning. I know she hates when I do that, but this is important.

"Fancy—"

"I know, I know. You don't want to see me in here, but we
need to talk. I'm in crisis!"

"No, it's not that—"

"Mrs. Washington, please! Just let me talk. Okay? Let me
get this all out. I stayed up all night trying to make the stupid
potion and I couldn't! Why did I lie to Rahim and tell him I
knew about Voodoo? I can't make chicken soup! How would I
know how to make a potion? What was I thinking?

"But really, it's not all my fault, right? I mean, it was wrong of him to assume that I know Voodoo just because I'm from Haiti. So doesn't some of the blame lie with him? Okay, okay. That's a stretch, but you have to help me! I need to find a way to fix this," I plead.

"Fancy—"

"Don't say that I have to tell him the truth, because I can't, okay? I've come too far to come clean now. He'll lose it if he finds out that all this time I was lying. He'll never look at me the same way if he finds out, so please, please, help me figure out a way to fix this."

Mrs. Washington doesn't reply. She just keeps looking over my shoulder with a mixture of regret and worry. I feel someone behind me before I turn around. . . .

Rahim is standing by the file cabinet holding a stack of plastic boxes. His eyes are dark with rage and hurt. My knees are weak, and it's only a matter of time before they fail me.

"The coach sent Rahim to my office to pick up the extra first-aid kits we had from last year," Mrs. Washington says slowly.

I swallow hard. This is all a horrible dream, and now would be a good time to wake up.

Wake up!

Rahim pulls the door open and storms out.

"Rahim, wait!"

I run after him and hear Mrs. Washington call out, "Fancy, there's something else. . . ." I can't hear the rest because I'm already down the hall. I grab his shoulder and he spins around, fire in his eyes.

"I can explain."

He bites his lower lip and looks at me as if I just plunged a dagger in his chest. "I don't want you to explain. I want you to say that you didn't lie to me."

"The thing is—"

"I don't want to know what 'the thing' is. I want to know if you lied to me after everything I told you."

There are a million thoughts racing around in my head. All the words I want to say are jumbled, and my body is so tight with guilt and anxiety, I'm practically vibrating.

"Rahim, listen. I didn't know that—"

"DID YOU LIE TO ME?"

I nod. "Yes, I lied to you. I don't know how to make a potion. I don't know anything about Voodoo or spells or anything. But I think that you and your dad—"

"Don't talk about my dad!"

"I know you're upset, but—"

"Upset? You're acting like you just stepped on my sneakers. You stood there and listened to me talk about my dad and how much I miss the way he used to be. You looked me in the eye and said you could help me! And this whole time you were just playing me?!"

"Rahim, I'm sorry. I don't know why I didn't just come out and tell you the truth."

He laughs sardonically. "I'll tell you why. You didn't tell me the truth because it would endanger your chances of going to that stupid party. That's all you care about. It doesn't matter who you have to lie to or push aside. You're willing to do anything just so you can be popular! Who the hell does that?!"

"Rahim, I'm sorry. I'm so sorry."

"I'm not stupid, Fancy. I knew the potion working was a long shot. But it was the only hope that I had. And you took it away. I'll *never* forgive you for that." He takes off down the hall and doesn't look back.

I place my hand over my mouth to try to stop the sobbing, but it doesn't help.

I hear laughter behind me. I turn to see who it is, and naturally, because the universe hates me, it's Imani.

"I knew it was only a matter of time. So that's how you did it, huh? You tricked him into pretending to like you. I hope the whole school doesn't hear about this," Imani says as she cackles and struts down the hall.

Moments after, the loudspeaker goes off. "Fancy Augustine, please report to Mrs. Washington's office. Fancy Augustine."

"Great! What now?" I shout.

I take my backpack and go to see Mrs. Washington. She's waiting for me in the hall just outside her office.

"Fancy, I wasn't here on Friday. But I didn't see anything from you in my school mailbox this morning. I also didn't get any files in my email. Can I take that to mean you didn't finish your assignments?"

"Rahim just broke up with me. I can't think about that right now!"

"I'm sorry to hear that. But schoolwork is not contingent on how your love life is working out," she reminds me.

I growl. "Fine. I'll get it done after school today, okay?"

"Unfortunately it's not."

"Fancy, get in here!" my mom's voice commands from inside the office.

No, this can't be!

But just one look at Mrs. Washington confirms my biggest fear. "My parents are here!"

"You didn't leave me much of a choice," she replies.

It feels like the breath has been ripped from my body. Mrs. Washington holds the office door open for me. I walk in and see my parents looking grave and seriously upset.

"Mom? Dad?"

My dad looks pensive. My mom looks like she's gonna blow any minute. My heart is at the bottom of my feet. My whole life flashes before me; it was too short, but there's nothing I can do about it now. It's over. *Fancy lived to the ripe old age of fifteen.*

My mom spits her words from between gritted teeth: "Sit down!"

Whatever horrors I thought awaited me in that office were nothing compared to what actually takes place. Mrs. Washington informs my parents of the long list of homework assignments I have missed, the number of classes I am on the verge of failing, and the countless times I have been scolded in class for not paying attention. The more they hear, the worse my mom's eye twitches. I'm so dead. Mrs. Washington goes on to tell them the reason why she thinks I've been so distracted.

"I believe Fancy is a very bright young woman, and I think she's capable of doing better than she is right now. But she's very distracted, and I think a major part of that is her social life."

"What social life?" my dad asks.

I look at Mrs. Washington and plead silently with my eyes. She looks at me as if to say she's sorry, and then: "Fancy has a boyfriend, and I think that relationship is pulling her focus. To be fair, she was distracted even before then, but now... She's giving everything she has to being a couple and not to her schoolwork."

"Boyfriend?! Fancy has a BOYFRIEND?!" My mom squeals loud enough to shatter glass.

Dad places a hand on Mom's shoulder to try and calm her down. "Wait, what about pre-SAT classes? She told us she was taking them."

"We have classes to help prep for the SAT, but those don't start for a few more weeks," Mrs. Washington says.

"I see," Mom says. Her voice is eerily calm now. That scares me more than her screaming. "So if you were not going to class after school, what were you doing? Spending time with the boyfriend you said you didn't have?"

"I'm sorry," I mumble.

"So you do have a boyfriend?" my dad says, sounding more hurt than angry.

"I don't— He— I... Yes. I had one. I'm not sure if he still likes me. I lied to him, and now he's really mad," I reply, not expecting my voice to crack the way it does.

Mrs. Washington goes on to tell them about all the after-school resources I could use that might help me get back on track. My parents don't say anything. The three of us are holding a conversation just with our eyes. It's tense and filled with misery; all I want to do is hide.

"Now, I can help you sign her up for—"

"Thank you, Mrs. Washington," Mom interrupts. "We appreciate all your help. But you won't need to sign Fancy up for anything—she's going back to Haiti to live with her grandparents. She lost her mind here in America. She's going back home to find it."

I would have been on the next plane to Haiti in the morning, but the flights were all booked up. The earliest one they could get was leaving the day after Imani's party. The delay doesn't stop Mom from spending the next few days packing up my stuff. She also takes away my laptop, iPad, and just about anything that needs to be plugged in. She only lets me have my computer long enough to do my homework. Before she got hold of my cell, I tried to call Rahim. I think he blocked me, because it kept going straight to voicemail. I tried him on all social media, and he's blocked me there, too. I know he's angry and won't ever take me back, but I just want to tell him how sorry I am. I'm sorry about so many things. How did I not hear the music playing? How did I not know that I was so close to being sent away?

When I see Rahim at school the next day, he glares at me and turns away. I'm sure he's heard that I will be going back to Haiti—the whole school knows. But Rahim doesn't care, doesn't so much as look at me when I see him in the halls.

Tilly knows I'm leaving. I can tell by how sad her eyes get when she sees me. I saw her standing by my locker, waiting to talk to me, but I ran away. I just couldn't face her.

Another person I avoid is Mrs. Washington. We met up in the hall and she asked me to come to her office, and I asked her if it was mandatory. She said it wasn't and that she just wanted to check on me. I glared at her and declined.

I go to class, where I continue to be made fun of because everyone thinks I tried to put a Voodoo curse on Rahim. I don't know how the story got so twisted, but I don't think it matters anymore.

When I get home that day, I go straight to my room or what's left of my room. There's just one thing left on the wall.

"White Jesus, I ruined everything. How do I fix it?"

And for the first time since I have known Him, White Jesus has nothing to say. It figures.

I go downstairs to get some water from the kitchen and hear voices coming from my parents' bedroom. Their door is slightly ajar. I peek in quietly and see my mom on the bed, sobbing in my father's arms.

"I don't want to send her away, but I don't know what else to do," she cries as he holds her.

I have never seen my mom cry. She's the boss of all of us. She's the toughest, and the one who always has it all together. And I made her cry.

I made my mom cry. . . .

CHAPTER
15

This whole time I worried that I would never get to be the girl on the cover of the romance book. The truth is that while I wasn't on the cover, I was definitely in the story—as the villain. I've done things in the past that made my parents mad—so mad that I'm sure they've been tempted to rethink their stance on day drinking. But this is the first time that I've actually hurt them.

Last night, hearing how shattered my mom was really got to me. I thought being sent back to Haiti for acting out was the worst thing that could happen, but I was so wrong. The looks on their faces are far worse than any punishment they could dish out. Now, thanks to me, there's a chill in the house. I managed to suck out all the warmth that used to be here.

How did I manage to mess up so spectacularly?

I lost my friendship with Tilly for no good reason. I had a million chances to make up with her, and I wasted all of them. Mrs. Washington looked genuinely disheartened when she learned about the many, many lies I had been telling. And there's the matter of Rahim. When I found out how much the potion meant to him, I should have just been straight with him. And now I've hurt, pissed off, and alienated everyone I care about. I did all this for a party. The very party I will never get to attend. Don't get me wrong, I know I don't deserve to go, but that doesn't make it hurt any less. Just thinking about the party brings a series of images to my head: the dress I would have worn, the life-altering entrance I would have made, the look on Imani's face when I outshined her...

"ARGH!!!"

I hear someone cough.

It's White Jesus.

"What is it?" I ask Him out loud.

He scans me with far more judgment than I'm used to—even from Him. It's like He's saying, *Figure your life out!*

"How? I can't fix this."

He rolls His eyes. I think He gets that from me.

"You're right. Maybe I can't fix it, but I should at least try."

The pushy little poster mumbles, *Finally.*

I know WJ is right. I made mistake after mistake, and now

I need to make up for it. So, like a disgraced YouTube star, I'm going on a Taylor Swift–sized apology tour.

My first stop is Mrs. Washington's office, but she's not in. So, I place a gift basket by her door. It contains two boxes of two-ply tissues, a large bottle of aspirin, and a bag of candy corn. On the card I wrote: *So you are armed and ready for next year. Sorry I was such a pain.*

I am just about to walk away when I see her coming down the hall. "Fancy, did you need something?" she says.

"I was just dropping this off." I pick up the gift basket leaning on the door and hand it to her.

"I'm surprised you didn't just let yourself in," she quips.

"I was tempted, but I figure since this is my last time in your office and I'm already in so much trouble, it might be prudent to skip breaking and entering."

"Good thinking." She looks inside the basket and grins. "Thank you! This is very thoughtful. Come in."

I follow her into the office and take my usual seat. She sits across from me. We're right back where we started. I recall all the time I spent in this office. I think I was here more often than I was in class.

"How are you?" she asks sincerely.

"I had bacon and eggs this morning. I think they were

sneering at me. The same could be said for my glass of OJ and the toast. Who knew breakfast foods were so judgy?" I ask.

"I'm sorry about that. I hope the next meal you have is more agreeable."

"Thanks."

She takes a deep breath and searches for something positive to make the situation better. "Well, at least you got to come to school and say goodbye to everyone. Fancy, I think everything is going to work out for you. I really do believe that."

"Optimist until the very end, huh?"

"Yes. And you should be, too," she insists with a warm, caring tone.

I shake my head. "I'm already deeply committed to pessimism. It's too late to turn back now."

"What about Tilly? How are you two?"

I don't reply, but the look on my face tells her everything she needs to know. "And should I ask about Rahim...?" she says gingerly.

I give her the same look. She nods with understanding. "With you gone, I'm not sure how I'll spend most of my days. It's going to be strange not to have to talk you off a ledge every five minutes."

"I know. I'm like twenty 'Weeping Wednesdays' wrapped up in one. Now you're off the hook. You don't have to bother with me anymore."

She rolls her eyes at me playfully. "You were never a bother. You know that."

I feel a lump forming in my throat and decide to get up and go before I lose it completely.

Mrs. Washington comes from around the table and actually gives me a hug! I embrace her in return and now I am really in danger of crying. I pull back. "I know what I'm gonna do first when I get back to Haiti."

"Oh really? And what's that?"

"I'm gonna go find Jean-Louis. We'll do a duet. Maybe start a band."

"Good plan," she lies.

"Oh, and thanks for not telling my parents about the Voodoo stuff under my bed."

"I figured that could stay just between us," she says. I smile sadly and walk out of her office for the last time.

It doesn't feel right to leave without saying goodbye to Tyson, and I don't want to put it off. So during lunch I go looking for him. I find him sitting on the bleachers studying his cell. He has the same intense look he had the last time we played *Mario Kart*. I take a seat next to him and peek at his screen. He's playing some racing game I've never seen before.

"Careful, you're gonna crash!" I warn him.

"No, I got this!" he says as he motions from side to side, determined to get past the car next to him. Suddenly, a barricade comes out of nowhere. The car hits it and flips over.

"Damn! I had it!" he shouts.

"Sorry," I reply.

He grumbles a little and then says, "It's cool. I have one more chance before the game resets."

I scoff. "Can I get a reset, too?"

"Yeah, Rahim told me what went down with you two. You messed up bad," he says, putting his cell in his back pocket. "You really lied about the whole Voodoo thing?"

I nod slowly. "I did."

"I expected better from you, Fancy." He sounds like a disappointed parent.

"I know. It was the stupidest thing I've ever done."

"Are your parents really sending you back to Haiti? Or are you just trying to get out of a rematch for *Mario Kart*?"

"Oh please, Rahim's little sister can take you," I tease.

"Asia? Don't let that cute face fool you; she's ruthless. I've played with her before. She cheats."

"Maybe. Or maybe she's just better at it."

Tyson shakes his head. There's a mix of admiration and wonder on his face. I have no idea why.

"What is that look for?" I ask.

"I was just thinking. You got the whole school to think you were a Voodoo witch. I gotta tell you, I'm torn—on one hand, that's foul as hell. But on the other hand, keeping up a lie that big...I'm a little impressed."

"Well, you're the only one. Everybody hates me," I reply, blinking back tears.

"Have you talked to 'everybody'?" he asks.

I shake my head. "He won't talk to me."

"Yeah, you did him real dirty. I've never seen Rahim so mad before," he admits. "At practice he slammed the ball so hard into the hoop, I thought he was gonna break the backboard."

I exhale deeply. "Leave it to me to send people to new levels of rage." I turn to look at him. "Anyway, I just came to say goodbye." I give him a quick hug, and it surprises him a little. He hugs me back.

"You can't change your parents' minds?" he asks when we part.

"That's never gonna happen. Hey, can you do me a favor?"

He shrugs. "What's up?"

"Make sure that Rahim is...okay?"

"Yeah. I got this," he says in his usual self-assured, cocky manner. I nod and walk away. He quickly catches up to me and blocks my path. "Look, I can't sell out my boy and tell you stuff he said to me. I'm loyal like that. But to be real, Rahim was different after you two started going out. He was better. Like the family stuff didn't get to him as much. And he talked about you all the time."

"He did?"

"Yeah. So, keep trying."

When I get back from school, I think my mom is expecting me to complain about not being allowed out without her permission and having limited internet access. But I don't do that. I've already hit bottom—no need to look for a subbasement.

Mom was also waiting for me to complain about the extra chores I was given. But I don't. In fact, I get right on the dishes after dinner without her needing to remind me. I also sweep and mop the kitchen floor. I never do as good a job as her, but it came out pretty decent.

I put in a load of laundry while I vacuum the living room. There was nothing fun or even slightly romantic about doing the chores, but there was some small solace in knowing I wasn't a total lost cause as a daughter.

Later that evening, I enter the newly spotless kitchen to get some water before bed. My mom is there, making tea. Her cell dings. I know the sound of that ding; it alerts her that a new murder podcast episode has just come out. I'm hoping she'll ask me to listen with her—if not tonight, then maybe tomorrow. But she doesn't. I guess we don't do that anymore.

So far, doing a bunch of chores has taught me three things: I'm excellent at folding copious amounts of laundry, dust is an ever-present threat, and trying to get grease off a plastic bowl requires no less than an act of God.

Every night when I'm done with housework, I want to crash, but I fight against it. Instead, I push myself to complete yet another school assignment. I know it doesn't matter now since I'm leaving, but I need to prove to myself that I can follow through.

I finally finish all my overdue homework, with just three days to go before my flight. That means that after doing dishes, I can actually get some non-school-related reading in. I'm about two chapters into my book when Mom enters my room.

"Ms. Dorcy came to me at choir rehearsal and wanted to talk about you. She wanted to compliment me on raising such a polite and kind child. And Mrs. Washington called me early this morning to say that she has faith in you. She believes you are capable of making better decisions."

"She has to say that, Mom. She's on my payroll," I reply with a small smile.

"Hmph," is all she says.

Later, I overhear her and Dad in the kitchen, debating whether they're doing the right thing. I can hear how torn Mom is about sending me away.

I enter and reassure her. "Mom, it's okay. I get why I'm going back. I'll be fine."

She clears her throat, nods, and hurriedly walks out of the room. I think she feared that if she stayed one moment longer, she'd openly weep.

It's my last day of school. This time tomorrow, I'll be headed back to Haiti. I wait for Tilly by the lockers, but she never comes. I get it.

I'm about to go to my last class when I hear my name called out on the loudspeaker. I'm told to report to Mrs. Washington's office. I'm not sure what I did. I don't recall causing any trouble between home and school today.

I enter the office that is basically my second home, and Mrs. Washington and my parents are waiting for me. I ask if they are here to sign me out officially. They tell me to have a seat.

"Fancy, your parents came here to consult with me about the possibility of you staying. They wanted to know if I thought you deserved another chance," Mrs. Washington says.

My jaw drops. I try to talk but words don't make it past my lips. I'd like to think she fought for me, but I haven't really given Mrs. Washington much of a reason to be my cheerleader.

"Fancy, did you hear me?" she asks.

My head and neck still work, so I nod.

"I told them that you have not been living up to your potential at all. But that I still held out hope for you."

"You did?!" I ask, not sure I heard correctly.

"I did. But as you know, the decision lies with them. I'll leave you three alone to talk."

Mrs. Washington excuses herself and says she'll be right outside the door.

My dad nudges my mom, who clears her throat. "Your father thinks that you are starting to see where you went wrong these past few weeks. He thinks that we should give you another chance to stay in the US."

I turn to Dad. "Really?"

"Maybe. Wait. There's more," he says.

Mom continues, "We are extremely upset with you and the way you've handled yourself. I don't trust you right now, and neither does your father. However, you appear remorseful."

"I am, I really am! I swear!"

"Well, saying it is not the same thing as behaving like it. We have not canceled your flight," she says.

My heart splits open.

"However, we have delayed it," Dad adds.

"Until when?" I ask.

"You have six months to show us that you now understand how important your education is and how serious we are about you being a good student," Mom replies. "We didn't come from as far as we did and sacrifice as much as we have just to have you throw it all away."

"So...you're giving me a second chance? I can stay?" I ask in a high-pitched voice, filled with anxiety.

My parents look at each other, and Dad nods in my direction.

"Yes. You can stay—" Mom says.

I leap out of the chair and hug them so tight, I'm pretty sure they can't breathe. I'm not sure how many times I say, "Thank you."

"Now, about you and boyfriends," Dad says.

"You can't have one. You're too young," Mom says sharply.

"However...," Dad adds, gently touching Mom's knee. He signals for her to speak. She's reluctant but eventually chimes in.

"You may have a guy friend that you can hang out

with—but only in a group. No school nights. Nothing after dark. And there will be no parties without adult supervision."

Before I can reply, Mrs. Washington enters. "They said I can stay!" I shout.

She smiles, "Yes, I know. But your parents and I conferred, and there are rules that must be followed from now on: I'll email your teachers a progress report at the end of every week. They'll sign off on it. I'll contact your parents immediately if the report shows you are falling behind. Also, all homework assignments must be handed in on time, no exceptions or extensions. Lastly, you are going to take these pre-SAT classes you lied about. Is that understood?" she asks.

"Yes. Understood."

Mrs. Washington addresses my parents. "Mr. and Mrs. Augustine, I truly believe Fancy's going to take school seriously, in a way she never has before. Isn't that right, Fancy?"

"One hundred percent!" I reply a little too eagerly.

"Obviously it's up to your parents to decide if you can go to Imani's party or not." Mrs. Washington looks at my mom. "Mrs. Augustine, if you do let her go, I can promise you that there will be adult supervision."

My parents exchange looks of uncertainty. "Who are these adults?" Mom asks.

"Imani's parents will be there. Imani's a straight A student, and they're diligent about keeping it that way. They would never let the party get out of hand. Also, two additional parents have volunteered to help chaperone."

Dad looks over at Mom; she nods slightly. "Okay."

What just happened?

"Really? I can go?!"

"Yes," Dad says.

Mom sighs but mumbles, "Yes, you can go."

"Wait, I don't have anyone to go with."

Mrs. Washington flashes me a cryptic smile. "You never know."

After I say goodbye to my parents, I float back to my locker. I get to stay! I really get to stay!

My joy turns to shock when I reach my locker and find Rahim waiting for me.

"Hey," he says softly.

"Hi." My voice is so high-strung that I don't even recognize it.

"So...my dad got the message you sent."

Crap.

"Ah, yeah. Sorry. I just wanted to help."

He takes out his cell and reads the email out loud:

Dear Mr. Robinson,

My name is Fancy. I hope you don't think I'm
out of line for this. But when Rahim talks
about you, I can hear in his voice how much he

misses you, and the way you used to be before your wife left. I also met your little girl, and I think Asia misses you, too. As an avid romance reader, I understand the urge to escape real life. But we can't hide in books or in our despair forever. I sent you a link to our school calendar. On it you'll find the schedule for all your son's basketball games. I'm not sure how to fix heartbreak. But maybe it starts with a basketball game and a fancy tea party....

Sincerely,
Fancy M. Augustine
PS: I owe you a tie.

I groan at how pathetic my email must sound. "I thought he needed to be reminded of what he still has. I'm sorry if sending the email was the wrong thing to do."

"Yesterday, I was on the court, in the middle of a game, and I made a basket. Suddenly, I heard, 'Yeah, that's my boy!' I thought I was imagining it, but nope, he was there. My dad hasn't come to my games since my mom left."

I perk up with a jolt. "He came?! That's great!"

He smiles. "Yes. And he even brought my sisters along. It was a family event. And for the first time in a year, my dad didn't keep looking around to see if my mom was gonna show up. He focused on us and not on her disappearing act. I got my dad back for a whole night. Next week, we're gonna talk to some therapist lady—as a family. It's a start, right?"

I nod enthusiastically. "Hell yeah! That's wonderful! I'm so happy for you!"

"We lost the game, but if you saw the way my whole family was cheering, you'd think we won." He adds, "Also, my dad said to tell you the tea party is scheduled for the first Saturday next month. And yes, Asia is making him wear the hat!"

"Wow, okay. I'm there."

"And get this: Ms. Dorcy is coming! Asia insisted her new piano teacher attend the big event. Ms. Dorcy's making strawberry cupcakes, and she's packing them all up in a big container of Tupperware to bring them over on the day."

"Wait, did you—"

"Yup, I warned my dad: All Tupperware must be returned within forty-eight hours. No exceptions!"

We laugh and then both go quiet.

"Guess what?"

"You're not going back to Haiti anymore," he says.

"How did—"

"I talked to Mrs. Washington earlier, and she hinted that maybe you might get to stay."

"I'm on probation but yeah, I get to stay."

"I'm sorry if I got you in trouble in any way. Seriously, my bad."

"Nope, it was all me, and I hope to make it up to you someday," I reply.

He takes my hand in his. "You already did."

"So...we're okay? You don't hate me?" I ask, holding my breath.

"No. I never did. I was just mad that you lied to me, but I could never hate you."

I squeal. "I've missed you so much!"

"Yeah, me too."

I eagerly reach out for a hug. He holds me close, and I hug him back. It feels nice, but I make sure it's a quick hug. I can't get in trouble again.

When we pull apart, I tell him my other news. "I actually get to go to the party. Do you...um...I mean...Can we go together?"

He hangs his head and exhales deeply, like he's bracing for something. "I said I would take you, and I still want to—as friends."

"I don't understand," I admit.

"I can't be with someone I don't trust."

I close my eyes and feel a warm stream of tears make their way down my face. "Oh. Got it. Makes sense."

"I'm sorry. I don't want to hurt you."

I wipe my face and nod slowly. It turns out all the other times I thought I was hurting were just a trial run for the real thing.

"Fancy, I need to know if that's good enough—a friendship. If it's not, I understand."

I can't feel my heart beating in my chest. There's a good chance it's simply just not working anymore.

"Fancy?"

"Just friends? I can do that," I reply.

"Okay, so we're good?" he asks.

"Sure!" I lie.

"I'll go home and change and pick you up later," he says, walking away. I wipe my eyes and try to commit to the simple act of breathing....

CHAPTER 16

Since Imani's party is later today, I try to focus on the fact that I get to go and not dwell on Rahim wanting to be just friends. Imani will have heard about our argument. She'll know it was never real in the first place. But I'm pretty sure I can spin a lovely tale of how we ended up really falling for each other. So I think I'm covered. Also, I don't have the dream dress I saw online, but I found something in my closet that should work well enough. I'm just glad I get to go. And Rahim and his dad are doing better, so I couldn't be happier.

There's only one thing missing....

It feels wrong that Tilly and I aren't getting dressed for this party together. I called her many times and texted but haven't gotten anything back. I hope she found a head-turning dress that would make Wednesday Addams proud. I take solace in knowing I'll see her there. Maybe it'll be harder for her to ignore me in person.

I look at myself in the mirror. I'm wearing a simple light-blue A-line dress. I won't stop traffic in this, but still, not bad. I just got my hair done—long, dark-brown goddess locs, with wine-colored highlights.

"So, White Jesus, what do You think?"

Before WJ can reply, someone knocks on the door. I ask who it is. "It's me," the voice says.

I open the door. "Mom?"

Hold on, did my mom just knock on my door?

She must be reading the shock on my face. "Do not get used to it. I still have the right to come in whenever! But your father suggested you should have a little more privacy. I'll try to knock more often."

I suppress a smile and push back the desire to scream with joy. I don't want her to second-guess the whole knocking thing. I just smile and mutter, "Thank you."

She enters and looks me over. She tells me I look nice but that something is off.

"Is it the earrings? Should I try a different pair?" I ask.

She shakes her head no. And then says she'll be right back. She returns holding a garment bag and hands it to me. "This is an early birthday present."

"No gift card this year?"

"You're turning sixteen, and you should get something special," she says with a glint in her eye. I unzip the bag and gasp: It's not just a dress—it's a gown—MY GOWN! It's the very same one I was drooling over this whole time! The shimmering pink ball gown is strapless and has tiny gems that sparkle like stars.

"How did you know I wanted this one?" I ask.

"When I took your laptop and your phone, I couldn't help but notice how many snapshots you had of the dress. Also, it was in your Amazon cart. I thought it would look perfect on you," she says. "Try it on!"

Mom helps me put it on and zip up the back. And together we look over the final results.

"Wow . . . ," she says.

"Thank you, Mom!"

Dad knocks, and we tell him to come in. When he sees me in my dress, he gets an odd look on his face. It's as if he's seeing me for the first time.

"Dad, what do you think?"

He blinks away tears.

"Dad, you okay?"

"What? Me? Yeah, I'm fine," he says, clearing his throat. "You look . . . Good job." He quickly walks away.

Mom shakes her head, amused. "On your wedding day, we're going to have to give him a sedative."

The dress was one thing, but when Mom hands me a small starter makeup kit, I'm pretty sure I'm dreaming. She helps me pick out a soft, muted rose lipstick and blush. And I even get to apply eyeliner! I look in the mirror.

I'm beautiful!

I know how fickle the mirror can be. I close my eyes, take a deep breath, and look again.

I'm still pretty!

Mirror, I think this is the beginning of a beautiful friendship....

The first thing I do when we pull up to the party is scan for Tilly, but I don't see her. I ask Rahim, but he hasn't spotted her, either. My heart sinks. I really wanted to see her. "So what do you think of this place?" Rahim asks. I look around and take it all in for the first time. Imani's house is a tasteful Colonial Revival with black trim. I know that from binge-watching *House Hunters* with my mom. The house has two large white pillars on each side of the entrance and a black Juliet balcony. Everything about the home is designed to let outsiders know that the residents are elegant and discerning.

Imani's mom is a world-renowned opera singer. She has performed all over, including the most prestigious opera house in the world, La Scala in Italy. I know because Imani has gone to great pains to make sure we all know. Her mom is currently doing a sold-out season with the Metropolitan Opera. Her dad is a high-powered entertainment attorney. I've seen him on TV a handful of times.

I look at the ornate white double doors. I'm officially mere yards away from reaching a new stratosphere of popularity.

I take Rahim aside and ask, "Is there ever an occasion that calls for a triumphant laugh? If there is, then this would be it!"

"Fancy, it's not that big a deal. It's just a party."

"Humph!" I reply, rolling my eyes.

"What? Fancy! Say what's on your mind."

"This is *just* a party to you because you've always been invited. Once you made it onto the basketball team, your entire high school life was laid out for you. You prequalify for everything. You don't know what it's like to be on the other side. You don't get to judge me if you've never experienced what it's like to be me."

"I get it, you want to be popular."

"No, it's not that. The world is big. There are only so many spotlights. I don't need to be center stage, but yeah, I'd like a little shine, too. I'd like to feel...liked. Wanted. Seen."

I take a step closer to him and admit what I've been trying to hide for a very long time. "Rahim, Imani's party is important to me. I know it's not supposed to be, but it is. So...can you be supportive? Please?"

He nods slightly and holds his hand out. "Yeah, I got you. And I'm being real with you—you look good as hell!"

I beam as he takes my hand again. We go toward the entrance.

"Fancy, you good?" Rahim asks, bringing me back to the present. I didn't realize I had stopped walking.

"Yeah, I was just thinking about Tilly."

"I think you two can work things out. I really do. You should try."

"Maybe. Let's just get through this moment, okay?"

"That's fair," he replies.

Standing guard at the door is a pretty white lady in her mid-thirties. Her dark blond hair is in a high ponytail. She's wearing an expensive-looking jacket and skirt set. She goes back and forth between the clipboard in her hand and the screen on her cell.

Rahim squeezes my hand and whispers, "You got this." I smile brightly back at him. My heart is beating at speeds that can't possibly be healthy. I reach out and place my hand on the double door. . . .

Rahim's cell goes off. He looks at his screen and says, "It's Tyson."

"Is he running late?"

"Nah, he's not coming, he had some family dinner thing he couldn't get out of. Hang on." He steps away from the line of kids waiting to get in.

You waited years to get inside those double doors; you can wait another sixty seconds.

Rahim comes back wearing a deep frown. Before I can ask him about it, the clipboard lady says, "Excuse me, if you two are not ready to enter . . ."

"No, we're ready, right?" I ask him.

"You should know what Tyson just told me," he says.

"What is it?" I ask. I catch Clipboard Lady glaring at me.

"He bumped into Tilly and her boyfriend at CVS. They were arguing. She accused him of trying to change her, and he accused her of being closed-minded. They were shouting and then Jason said he didn't think things would work out. He broke up with her right then and there."

"He *what*?"

Clipboard interrupts. "There's a welcome presentation scheduled in the great room. Ms. Parker asks that all her guests be present."

I look around. Everyone is now inside except for us.

I turn my attention to Clipboard. "One second. I just need to find out—"

"I'm sorry, but the hostess was very clear. Everyone must be present for the presentation. We are about to close the doors. Are you in or out?"

Rahim looks at me, not sure which way I'll go. I look at the double doors and then out at the path that leads to Tilly.

"I'll rock with you, no matter which way you want to go," Rahim promises. Once again, I look at the doors and the path to the exit.

"Hello? Are you coming?" Clipboard pushes.

I nod to Rahim, letting him know that I have made up my mind. "We're going inside," I tell her.

"Finally. Where's your invite?" she asks.

"Oh, it's right here...." I open my handbag and dig down to get the invite. I scoop up a bunch of junk along with the envelope: scraps of paper, gum wrappers, and a long, slim mascara wand.

The memory comes back to me in a vivid flash. It's so visceral it's like I was physically transported there. I hold the mascara up and recount to Rahim how Tilly and I used to pretend we were princesses. I tell him about the moment Tilly handed me my mom's mascara and said, "Princess, your sword."

"And from that point on, we slew dragons, witches, bandits...You name it. We were a team."

The tears welling up in my eyes make everything blurry. It's ironic; the worse my vision gets, the more clearly I see.

"Oh...I'm so stupid!"

"Fancy, what's wrong?" Rahim asks.

"If you have some kind of medical condition, you are obligated to let the homeowners know. We're not responsible for—"

"Cool it, Clipboard!" I say hotly.

She sneers, clearly offended.

I turn back to Rahim. "Tilly gave me my first weapon. It protected me not just from make-believe monsters, but the real-life ones too. And now that she needs me, I'm gonna ditch her for some silly party, thrown by the girl who hates me? Who does that?"

Rahim nods in agreement. "So...you wanna...?"

"Get the hell out of here and go check on my friend," I reply, filled with certainty.

"Wait!" Clipboard says. "Look, I don't like you or what I have known of you in the past few minutes. But this party is... top of the line. Are you sure?"

"Absolutely! I have a princess to rescue," I proclaim. I hand the woman the invite. Rahim and I turn around and walk back the way we came.

We're out on the street when I hear Imani's voice. "Where the hell do you think you're going?" she demands, both hands on her hips. I ask Rahim to please call a Lyft.

"Imani, I can't stay. Tilly needs me."

"I don't care what your pathetic little friend needs. You don't get to miss my event. Do you have any idea how many people would kill to be invited? Do you know what this party can do for your social life? How *dare* you even think about walking out?"

I've known Imani for years, and yet this is the first time I'm really seeing her. There's something behind her eyes, flawless makeup, and polished demeanor. She sounds angry and put out by my trying to leave, but it's more than that. She sounds desperate and needy. She *needs* someone she can make feel bad. Someone she can look down on. It's the only way she can be certain she's still on top.

What if she didn't wear the latest fashions, or came to school with no makeup? What would happen if she came to class and her hair wasn't runway ready? What happens when you keep telling the world you're perfect? Does the world force you to prove it every day? Isn't it exhausting?

"Hello? I'm talking to you! How dare you try and ditch my party!" she yells.

"I was so wrong. I threw away the best friendship I ever had for something that wasn't even real—the perfect teenage life. There's no such thing," I reply.

Her nostrils are flaring and her fists are balled up tightly. "Do not play with me, Falencia! I already told you, I am the goal."

I laugh because I finally, finally get it. "No, you're the cautionary tale."

Rahim calls out, "Lyft's here," as a black car turns the corner and stops in front of the house. He holds the door open for me. Imani follows us to the car. I take the mascara wand out of my purse and hand it to her. She takes it, although she's clearly not sure why I'm giving it to her.

"What's this for?" she asks.

"Slaying dragons. You can keep it. I don't need it anymore. I just slew mine."

She shouts out to me, "You can't leave!"

I laugh and share my new insight with her: "Imani, it's *just* a party."

The Lyft pulls over in front of Tilly's house, but I ask the driver to go around the back. I think I know exactly where she will be, and it's not inside her home. The driver makes a turn and drops us off at the backyard entrance.

"Are you sure she'll be out here? It's cold," Rahim says.

"Yeah, I'm sure," I reply, making my way to her backyard. I

head for the small toolshed. When we were kids, Tilly begged her parents to get her a little room of her own out here, so they let her have this storage shed. Tilly painted it dark blue with a black skull and crossbones on the door. She said that no one could enter unless she gave her permission. Her parents agreed, as long as Tilly promised not to build anything that would cause them to have to get a criminal attorney.

I'm the only one who knows what's inside. It's not what most people think. It's easy to suspect that Tilly's shed features an array of morbid odds and ends. Her parents have joked that she might be keeping a body in there. They would be shocked to know what Tilly really has behind the door. It's info that would damage her reputation if it ever got out.

It turns out our little Wednesday Addams is a huge—and I do mean huge—fan of Disney! Yes, she's into creepy, scary, and odd things. But she also has a Minnie Mouse collection that she's had since she was a toddler. Her parents think she got rid of all that kid stuff, but she didn't. And what started out as a small space to hide her favorite stuffed toys became a treasure chest of all the things she'll never admit to owning. I promised I would never tell anyone that Tilly adores basically anything Disney-themed and that she sometimes gets under her Goofy blanket when she feels scared and overwhelmed.

"You're right, there's a light on," Rahim says.

"Okay, I got it. Rahim...," I begin.

"I'll leave you two alone."

"I'm sorry tonight ended so...unceremoniously."

"I'm not," he says.

"Why? Aren't you the least bit upset that we didn't go to the party?"

"Nah, I like that you're the kind of person who has her friend's back. Go and see if you can cheer her up."

I give him a hug, and he takes off. I knock on the shed door.

"Mom, I don't want to talk! Please go away!" she says.

"Tilly...it's me," I reply, a surge of nervous energy rippling through me. *What if she won't talk to me? What if I can't make up for the horrible way I treated her?* "Tilly, please open the door."

"What do you want? You abandoned me, just like Jason did!"

"Well, open the door so you can punch me in the face. That's always an option," I joke.

I wait for a moment, but I don't hear her moving around in there. Maybe she won't open the door. I've really messed up this time. She needed me, and because of my obsession with Imani's dumb party, I let her down.

Luckily, I finally hear her walk toward the door and open it. I'm not sure what to expect when I see her standing in front of me. She looks pissed off. Her eyes are swollen from crying. Her nose is red, and her hair is a mess. The anger on her face tells me she just might take me up on my offer and deck me.

"Hi, Tilly."

She pauses to look me over. It seems like forever before

she makes her next move. She comes close and—falls into my arms, sobbing.

"Aww, it's okay. I promise, it's gonna be okay." I hold her close and blink away my own tears. We settle on the floor surrounded by all the stuffed animals and her cozy blanket. I know how to make Tilly feel better when she's down, but this is her first broken heart. Tilly continues to cry for a long while. I don't say anything or push her to talk. I just hold her against me and let her know that Goofy and me are there for her. She finally lifts her head and takes deep breaths in an attempt to calm down.

Suddenly, a thought occurs to her. "Wait, why aren't you at the party?"

I shrug. "I had more important places to be."

"Hold on, you ditched Imani's party for me?"

"Tyson told us about you and Jason. I had to come. It's the only right decision I've made concerning us in a while," I admit.

"I'm sorry you missed out on the party," Tilly says.

"Who cares? There were no dead bodies or fake blood. So wrong."

I finally get a small smile from her.

"Tilly, what happened?" I ask.

She tells me that prior to their trip to CVS, she and Jason were having lunch, and he told her to order something she didn't like. She ordered what he suggested but she resented him for it. He went with her to CVS to get some nail polish;

all the while she was fuming. Eventually she came out and told him how she felt. They argued and before she knew what was happening, she'd been dumped. Tilly starts crying all over again. She asks if she did something wrong. I assure her she didn't. She says she liked him a lot and can't understand why he dumped her. I gently take her face in my hands, making sure our eyes meet.

"Tilly, Jason rejected you because he couldn't handle dating a proud member of P3!" She looks at me, and I smile at her and add, "When you're dating a member of the Princess Protection Program, you don't get to treat that girl any way you want. Whoever dates a member of our group needs to come correct! And Jason knew he couldn't handle it."

"I almost forgot about that," she says, wiping her eyes.

"I didn't. I keep up with the union dues, every year," I tease. "Tilly, I'm sorry I messed up."

"We both did," she points out. "Oh, and I would like to reserve some time later—when I'm not a mess—to fawn over your dress. You look hot!"

I laugh. "I'll gladly add you to the reservation list. Do you have a picture of your dress?" I ask.

She shows me a selfie she took earlier. She's wearing a black, tea-length, empire-waist dress with a mesh sequin overlay.

"Tilly, you look spectacular!"

"I know, right?!" We both start laughing.

"So . . . are we good?" I ask carefully.

She places her hand on the side of my face. "Hell yeah— Wait!

I can hear the shed talking!" she says. She tries to listen really hard and then reports back. "The shed said, 'Tilly, I'm glad that pompous jerk is gone.'"

"Me too, shed!" I shout as if I'm talking to the room.

"Tell me all about Rahim. Did you kiss? You did, didn't you? OMG! You guys kissed and I missed it."

I tell her everything that happened between us: the good, the bad, and, yes, the super heartbreaking.

"I'm sorry, Fancy. Are you sure you two can be just friends?"

I shrug. "I'll get over my feelings for him soon enough. I mean, how long can heartbreak last? Three, four days?"

"Um, yeah. That sounds just about right," she lies.

Someone knocks on the shed door. Tilly goes to open it, but there's no one there. She comes back holding a large brown paper bag.

"Who was that?" I ask.

"I don't know, but they left this." We look inside it together. There are candy bars, chips, juice, a pint of ice cream, and a box of tissues.

"I think Rahim left it. Fancy, did you tell him to get all this stuff?"

"No."

"Well then, how did he know?" she asks.

My cell dings. It's a text from Rahim. I burst out laughing and show the text to Tilly:

Five sisters = superpower!

I can't help but smile.

"Fancy . . . ," she says, her eyes filling with tears. "It hurts."

I turn to Tilly and promise her that one day, she'll find a guy who deserves her.

She lies down and puts her head in my lap. I stroke her hair gently and vow that eventually things will be okay. We'll get to the treats, but for right now, we make good use of the tissues. . . .

CHAPTER 17

It's been nearly a month since that night in the shed with Tilly. She keeps asking me if I regret not going to the party, and I assure her that I don't. It hasn't been easy for her, but I can see she's coming out of her funk. She's working on a new horror dollhouse. She decided to do one she calls Heartbreak Hotel. It's a horror hotel featuring pissed-off ghost dolls and the exes they got revenge on. It's super creepy and, yeah, kind of awesome.

The four of us—Rahim, Tyson, Tilly, and me—hang out all the time now. We get along effortlessly and it's always fun. Every once in a while, I catch Rahim looking at me in a way that makes me think he wishes we were together. But I'm pretty sure that's just in my head. He made himself clear: He only wants friendship. I like us being friends, I really do.

But some small part of me aches for what we used to be. I miss holding hands and traveling the stars with him. I don't let the dull pain of our breakup get me down for too long. We're making the "just friends" thing work and that's enough. I'm not sure how I'll handle it when he starts seeing another girl, but for now, I'm managing my heartbreak.

At lunch one day, Tilly mentions she's entering her horror hotel into a dollhouse design contest. Tyson asks if she created a playlist for it.

"Really?" she says.

"You can't have a house of horror without a good soundtrack. Who raised you?" he asks, clearly offended.

It's not long before the two of them are plotting out death scenes and what track should be playing in the miniature speakers they install. I think there's something more between them than music and gore.

In the middle of my lunch period, I hear my name over the loudspeaker. I have been requested to report to Mrs. Washington's office.

Oh no . . .

The first thing I say when I open the door to her office is, "I am not guilty!"

She's sitting at her desk; she looks up and says, "Guilty of what?"

I shrug. "I don't know. I figure I should start working on my defense now," I reply.

"Come in and close the door behind you," she says. I don't like this. Wait, *did* I do something wrong? I try to search my mind, but so far, nothing.

I take a seat in my usual chair.

"Fancy, I've been feeling a little neglected lately. You haven't come to see me."

I'm not sure if she's joking or not. "Wait, that's good, right? It means I'm not in trouble?"

"Yes, that is good. But I missed you," she says with a pleasant smile.

"Yeah, I can see that. I'm your favorite student, aren't I?" I reply.

"You're okay to talk to, but I actually enjoy the more stimulating conversation I get from other students."

My jaw drops. The thick, decaying scent of betrayal lingers heavily in the air. It's only when I see the expression on her face that I know she's joking. "Wow, Mrs. Washington, didn't know you had it in you." She laughs, and I push it. "You know I'm your favorite. It's okay, Mrs. Washington, it'll be our secret."

"I will not confirm that any one student is my favorite. I

will, however, tell you that I am very proud of you for working so hard both at school and for being a real friend to Tilly."

"Yeah, you're right. But I gotta tell ya, I heard that Imani has the most beautiful grand staircase, just perfect for making an entrance. And while I no longer covet her life, is it okay if I daydream about her staircase? You know my small but elegant dream, right?"

"Yes, yes, I know. A grand staircase and a slow dance."

"But we put our dreams away," I reply.

"Are you still okay with your decision to miss the party?"

"I'm more than okay. You know, Mrs. Washington, Imani's party was just that—a party. You can't let that stuff dictate your whole life. It's not healthy," I tease.

"Yeah, well, that's great advice. I was just looking over your file, and it looks like your birthday is this weekend."

"Yes, I'll be sixteen. So life should have no more surprises in store for me. I've figured everything out. And now, I just want to skip ahead to the easiest part of all: bring on adulthood! I got this!"

She laughs at me. "Well, before you race toward the paradise that you think is adulthood, I wanted to give you a little something."

"What is it?" I ask.

"A good friend from college is part owner of a high-end event-planning firm. They handle fundraising for New York landmarks and institutions. I had lunch with her last weekend, and she told me about her new client. They own a large building in Manhattan. I thought you'd be interested in maybe taking a tour."

"Oh, that's nice. A tour of what?" I ask.

She looks up at the ceiling as if she's thinking really hard. "Um...I can't remember what the place is called. You might not even want to go. Anyway, she gave me two tickets. I'm giving you the other one. It's inside."

"Okay, cool. Thanks, Mrs. Washington," I reply. On my way out, I open the envelope.

And then run back into her office. I don't know that I'm screaming until she tells me to stop. "OMG!"

She chuckles. "Are you okay?"

"No, I'm not! This is a ticket to a private tour of the main branch of the New York Public Library! Including the secret apartments!"

"Fancy, I can't breathe!" she says. I hadn't even realized I was hugging her, but I guess I was. And now I refuse to let her go.

"Thank you, thank you, thank you!"

"Still can't breathe," she gasps.

"I'm sorry. There's a good chance I won't be able to let you go. But what a way to die, huh? Standing next to the girl who in less than forty-eight hours will be standing in the nexus of the universe!" I finally release her and thank her again as I dance out of her office. Best. Day. Ever.

Tilly comes over to my house to help me get ready for the library tour. Since we didn't get to wear our dresses to the party, we thought we should wear them somewhere else. So, I'm wearing mine to the event at the library tonight. And Tilly is wearing hers—for her first real date with Tyson! I worried that she would be overdressed, but apparently there's no such thing when you're attending a coffin expo. Tyson is really excited and has already created a playlist for their evening together.

I make Tilly promise to fill me in on all her first-date details when she gets back. We hug goodbye and she whispers in my ear, "Make sure you fill me in, too."

An hour later, Dad gives me a ride to the library. Mrs. Washington hasn't arrived yet and I'm glad, because I want to be here alone, just for a few moments. I've come to this place so many times, but never at night. The building is even more breathtaking. I'm standing in front of three stories worth of Vermont marble and ornate columns. I marvel at the glorious three-door archway and the water fountains on both sides named Beauty and Truth. And, of course, I take the time to appreciate the stone lions, Patience and Fortitude. I'm glad I dressed up; the majesty of this place simply demands it.

Mrs. Washington appears, accompanied by her event planner friend, Ashley. She makes a call and a few minutes later, a security guard appears and lets us inside. There's a tall, older man with gray hair and glasses waiting for us.

"This is William. He's going to be our tour guide." We greet him and I'm unable to hide my excitement.

"I'm dying!" I whisper to myself as I behold the full grandeur of the white marble entryway of Astor Hall. There are larger-than-life archways in every direction. The light from the massive crystal chandelier above hits the mineral floor, causing a shimmering effect. The ceilings feature colorful paintings that depict the evolution of the written word. This place is awe-inspiring. It really is the most romantic place in the world. I'll store up this moment and visit it in my head later. At that point, I'll add Rahim. I'll put him in a handsome suit and tie. I don't see him giving in and wearing dress shoes, but hey, it's my daydream, so I can dress him the way I want.

A guard takes our coats, and that's when Ashley and Mrs. Washington see my dress in full. They both tell me how much they love it. I admit it's over the top, but they disagree.

"I'm all for this look. You're stunning, Fancy," Mrs. Washington says.

"Thank you!"

"Shall we start the tour?" William asks.

"Yes!" I shout like the awful book nerd that I am. This must be how some people feel about shoe shopping.

"Okay, let's start here in Astor Hall," William says.

We tour all the collections of rare books. (I can't touch them, of course.) I also get to see the apartments that were created decades ago. No one lives there now. I ask Ashley, "Do you think the library would notice if a cute Black girl with an obsession with books quietly moved in?"

"Yeah, I think they might." She laughs.

The rest of the tour goes by quickly, and each moment is a dream. William tells us about all the work involved in preserving older books. And I get to see the room where Pulitzer Prize–winning writers give their speeches!

As our tour guide wraps up, Ashley asks me if I had a good time.

"I don't even have words."

"I think Fancy will remember this for a long time, thank you, William," Mrs. Washington adds.

"My pleasure," he replies as he waves good-bye and makes for the exit.

I turn to leave as well, but Mrs. Washington tells me to wait. She nods toward Ashley.

"Fancy, remember when I said I had two tickets to this private tour?" she asks.

"Yeah, why?"

"Well, I actually had three. Two for us and one for..."

She trails off.

"Who?" I ask, looking around.

"Why don't you turn the corner and find out?" Mrs. Washington suggests.

I'm not sure what's going on, but I do as she asks. I turn the corner, where I'm greeted by a grand staircase.

Suddenly, the space is filled with soft, romantic music. The lights slowly spin, making the once-charming space downright enchanting.

"Mrs. Washington?" I ask, still uncertain.

She nods and tells me to keep walking. I joke as I get to the staircase, "The music, the lights, the books...This moment would actually be perfect if—"

The words die in my mouth because standing there, at the bottom of the grand staircase...is Rahim.

I try to talk but can't. He's dressed in an actual suit and tie! He looks dashing and sexy beyond words. Is this really happening? It can't be, can it?

He takes me in and whispers under his breath, "Wow..." My heart flutters out of control, and I blink back tears.

"Hi," he says.

"Hi," I mouth, unable to find my real voice.

As I descend the staircase, Rahim comes halfway up the steps and holds out his hand to guide me down.

"I don't...What's happening?" I ask incredulously.

"Tyson was at my house while I was on the computer. He looked over my shoulder and pointed out that most of my search history has to do with you. He also remarked that I talk about you even more now than I did when we were together. And last week, this came in the mail...."

He takes something out of his pocket and shows it to me.

"You got a library card?!" I ask, squealing like a kid.

"Yes," he says begrudgingly. "It's stupid because I'm probably never gonna use it. And if I need a book, I'll just download it. But I got it because...if you're going to the nexus of the universe, this was my ticket to go with you—as your boyfriend. If that's still something you want?"

I bite my lower lip to keep from grinning so wide. "Yes. I still want that," I whisper. He holds me close; we begin to dance....

He's graceful and light on his feet. He notes the shock on my face. "Sanctimonious sneakerheads are full of surprises," he jokes. "Fancy, you're gorgeous."

"Thank you! This is like a dream. Wait! *Is* this some kind of dream I'm having? I mean, I'm not gonna wake up and find out I'm late for school, right?"

He shakes his head. "If this were a dream, would I be wearing these on my feet?"

I look down, and I don't know how I missed it, but—Rahim is wearing Jordans! I laugh uncontrollably. In a dream I would never put him in sneakers with an outfit like that! This is the real deal!

"I'm sorry," he begins. "I know a guy in a romance book would never wear—"

"I don't care what the guy in the romance book does. He can't compare to the guy I found in the real world. What about you? Is there some fiery planet you'd rather be on right now?"

He gazes back at me. "Nah. I'm good right here, with you."

He leans in, lips parted, and kisses me. We slow dance in the center of the public library, surrounded by stories of love lost and love found. It's then that I realize great romances don't just happen in books—every once in a while, they make it out into the real world. And sometimes, they even happen to girls like me.

Stephanie Gerard

MARIE ARNOLD

was born in Port-au-Prince, Haiti, and
came to the United States at the age
of seven. She grew up in Brooklyn,
New York, alongside her extended
family, and attended Columbia College
Chicago with a focus on creative
writing. Marie is a *New York Times*
and *USA Today* bestselling indie
author under the name Lola StVil. She
is also the author of *I Rise* and *The
Year I Flew Away*.